Wedding Deal with Her Rival

Kate Hardy

HARLEQUIN

Romance

HARLEQUIN

Romance

Recycling programs
for this product may
not exist in your area.

ISBN-13: 978-1-335-59652-9

Wedding Deal with Her Rival

Harlequin Enterprises ULC
22 Adelaide St. West, 41st Floor
Toronto, Ontario M5H 4E3, Canada
www.Harlequin.com

Printed in U.S.A.

Kate Hardy has been a bookworm since she was a toddler. When she isn't writing, Kate enjoys reading, theater, live music, ballet and the gym. She lives with her husband, student children and their spaniel in Norwich, England. You can contact her via her website, katehardy.com.

Books by Kate Hardy

Harlequin Romance

A Crown by Christmas
Soldier Prince's Secret Baby Gift

Reunited at the Altar
A Diamond in the Snow
Finding Mr. Right in Florence
One Night to Remember
A Will, a Wish, a Wedding
Surprise Heir for the Princess
Snowbound with the Brooding Billionaire
One Week in Venice with the CEO
Crowning His Secret Princess
Tempted by Her Fake Fiancé

Visit the Author Profile page
at Harlequin.com for more titles.

To Archie and Dexter,
best Edit-paw-ial Assistants ever.

Praise for
Kate Hardy

"Ms. Hardy has written a very sweet novel about forgiveness and breaking the molds we place ourselves in...a good heartstring novel that will have you embracing happiness in your heart."
—*Harlequin Junkie* on *Christmas Bride for the Boss*

CHAPTER ONE

WILL YOU MARRY ME? Catriona tried the words out in her head.

They sounded utterly wrong.

But she didn't have any other option. She'd analysed every line of her grandfather's will, and his lawyer had made it watertight. Whatever Catriona chose to do, she'd become Viscountess of Linton; under Scots law, the oldest child inherited the title, regardless of gender. But, if she didn't get married in the next six months, then under the terms of James Findlay's will the castle and the estate would be split between her three half-brothers—and she'd get nothing.

She sighed.

This wasn't about greed. She couldn't care less about the money. But she did care about the castle; it was the one place where she'd been happy when she'd been growing up. She knew that Tom, Lachlan and Finn wouldn't look after Lark Hill Castle. They didn't know the place or feel about it the way she did. Under the guidance of their mothers, they'd simply sell the property and land to the highest bidder, not bothering about what happened to the tenants or the people who worked on the estate—or to the castle itself. She hoped that her misgivings were ill-founded but, if her fears were right and they followed in their father's footsteps, every last penny would be gone within a year.

James Findlay—the Fourteenth Viscount of Linton, to give him his correct title—had known that Catriona would be a safe pair of hands and would see herself as the custodian of Lark Hill. If she inherited the castle, the tenants would all keep their homes and get their roofs fixed; everyone would keep their jobs; and she'd also find a way of making the estate look after itself to the point where she'd be able to give the boys something to help them set up their future. At least, that was her plan.

So why, why, *why* had Gramps put that ridiculous clause in the will to say that she had to get married, first?

He knew how she felt about marriage.

Her parents had married eight times between them, for pity's sake. If her father hadn't died ten years ago, there would've been at least two more. Thomas Findlay seemed to have suffered from a bad case of five-year itch after his divorce from Catriona's mother, divorcing, remarrying and producing another child roughly every five years. Catriona's mother was on her fifth divorce.

And then there had been Catriona's own mistake, seven years ago, when she'd got engaged to Mr Very Wrong. Thankfully she hadn't actually married Luke, but the way her engagement had imploded had destroyed her last vestiges of belief in romantic love. As far as she was concerned, 'love' was simply a marketing device designed to sell cards, flowers and little cutesy knick-knacks that nobody really wanted. It certainly didn't last. Thanks to her parents and Luke, she'd learned her lesson—and she'd learned it well.

With her elbows propped on her desk and her chin resting on her interlinked fingers, Catriona stared at the will, her eyes narrowed. She had to be married within six months of the reading of her grandfather's will. Though the will itself didn't specify how long the marriage had to last. Or that she had to be in love with her husband… So it didn't technically have to be a *real* marriage.

In which case, all she had to do was find the perfect husband. Someone who would agree to marry her for, say, a year—and then walk away with everything he'd brought into the marriage and nothing from Lark Hill.

All the men she knew outside work were either married or in a serious relationship with one of her own friends, so they weren't suitable. That left her colleagues. The ones she'd consider trusting to do the job were already married.

Except one: Dominic Ferrars. And he was the last person she could ask.

Not because she didn't trust him; he definitely had integrity. Though most people became corporate lawyers because of the high salary. Was that what drove him? She knew Dominic was an ambitious workaholic, and he was in the running for the next partnership in the legal firm where they both worked. As was she, on both counts: which was probably why they tended to rub each other up the wrong way, she thought wryly. Asking him for help would feel beyond awkward. How would she react if their positions were reversed and he asked her to marry him for a year? If she were honest with herself, she'd probably scoff in amused disbelief.

But, try as she might, she couldn't think of any other man she could ask to be her temporary husband.

Hating having to ask for such a personal favour, but knowing that the future of Lark Hill and the tenants depended on her, she typed out an email. Then she deleted it, rewrote it, deleted it again, and finally settled on:

Are you free for a business discussion at some point in the next week? Half an hour should be enough. Suggest over lunch. Thanks, CF.

She stared at the message glumly for a few more seconds, then sighed and pressed 'send'.

A business discussion? Over lunch?

Dominic Ferrars stared at the email, puzzled. What business could Catriona Findlay possibly want to discuss with him outside the office? And actually taking time for lunch? She usually ate a sandwich at her desk while she dealt with paperwork. He was pretty sure it couldn't be anything to do with the partnership race; she was as ambitious and competitive as he was, and she'd want to win the position on merit.

Which left…what? The more he thought about it, the less of a reason he could pinpoint.

There was only one way to find out. And he was intrigued enough to do it. He replied.

12.30 today, Luigi's? DF

The Italian sandwich bar just round the corner from their office sold excellent coffee and even more excellent paninis. More to the point, they'd be able to find a quiet table there and discuss whatever this 'business' was.

His email pinged again.

Thank you. See you there. CF

He concentrated on paperwork and put the meeting out of his mind until twelve-twenty. And then he made sure he was at Luigi's for half-past twelve on the dot.

So was Catriona. Wearing her usual navy business suit, crisp white shirt, and the kind of shoes that looked elegant but he'd just bet she could run in them if she needed to. She wore minimal make-up, no jewellery apart from a practical watch and a very discreet pair of pearl studs in her ears, and her dark hair was cut in a sleek, shiny bob. The whole image screamed expensive lawyer with a razor-sharp mind: which was exactly what she was. And he pushed aside the fact that she was also really pretty. That wasn't relevant and he wasn't even going to think of her in those sort of terms.

'Thank you for coming to meet me, Dominic,' she said. 'Lunch is on me. No strings,' she added swiftly.

Dominic inclined his head in acknowledgement. 'Thank you.' She was carrying a slim satchel-style briefcase, so clearly she'd brought either documents or a laptop with her. He wondered again why she hadn't simply spoken to him before or after work in the office. 'I'm intrigued by this "business" discussion.'

For a second, she looked intensely uncomfortable. *Interesting*. Catriona Findlay wasn't easily flummoxed. This must be something big.

'Let's order, and then we can discuss it,' she said.

'Sure.'

Once they'd ordered—and why wasn't he surprised that she drank plain black coffee rather than a frothy cappuccino?—they found a quiet table.

Close up, he could see that her eyes weren't quite the piercing ice-blue he'd always thought they were; the edge of her irises were almost navy. In other circumstances, and if she were any other woman, he'd admit to the attraction and maybe ask her out to dinner. But this was Catriona Findlay, who intimidated most of the lawyers he knew. She didn't suffer fools at all, let alone gladly.

So instead he waited for her to start the conversation.

'Thank you again for agreeing to meet me,' she said.

As openings went, it was polite enough. But he'd noticed the fleeting expression in her eyes that said she really didn't want to be having this conversation.

Curiouser and curiouser, he thought. This definitely felt like an *Alice in Wonderland* moment. 'You said half an hour,' he mused, doing his best to look casual but watching her very closely indeed.

'Yes. So I'll cut to the chase,' she said, and took a deep breath. 'Will you marry me?'

What?

Was he going mad? Had he just dropped into some weird parallel universe? Or had his fiercest rival for the next partnership in their firm just asked him to marry her?

Dominic stared at Catriona, too stunned to answer.

Marry her?

According to the office grapevine, she dated even less frequently than he did. All her energies went into her job—a job that she did extremely well, to be fair, and any legal firm would be lucky to have her as a partner.

Why would a woman so totally focused on her career want to get married?

And, more specifically, why did she want to get married to *him*?

Marriage wasn't on his agenda. Not when his goal was to become partner of a top London law firm. By concentrating on his career, he'd ensure he earned enough so his family never had to struggle again.

'I take it that your silence means no,' she said. 'OK. Thanks for your time, and I'm sorry for wasting it.'

Just as she was getting up to leave, he found his voice. 'Hold on. Firstly, our lunch hasn't arrived yet. And, secondly, you haven't heard my answer.' Where had that come from? It sounded almost as if he were about to say yes. 'Which is "why?",' he added swiftly.

For a long, long moment, she paused. And then she sat down again. 'This is a confidential discussion,' she said.

'Then why didn't you book one of the meeting rooms at work?'

'I…' She looked blank.

Whatever this was about, it had really disconcerted her. Even though he didn't really like her very much, he could sympathise with the fact that she was clearly in a tricky situation and was finding it hard to ask for help. 'As you said, it's confidential. I'll respect that,' he said.

'Thank you.' She took a deep breath. 'It's complicated.'

He'd expected better from her. She was good at cutting to the chase. 'Give me the short version,' he said, knowing she'd see it as a challenge.

'I need to get married,' she said, 'to fulfil the conditions of a will.'

He scoffed. 'Which is the plot of just about every soppy romantic movie going.'

She raised an eyebrow. 'And you know this because you watch a lot of soppy romantic movies?'

There was the quick and slightly acerbic wit she was known for. 'No. My sisters do.'

'It's also very Jane Austen,' she said, her eyes narrowing to ice-blue slits. 'Marriage and inheritance is pure *Pride and Prejudice* territory. So you can drop the intellectual snobbery. Not that there's anything wrong with soppy romantic movies.'

Was she saying that *she* liked soppy romantic movies? No way. Dominic would've pegged her as someone who watched French art-house films and didn't need the subtitles. Maybe Catriona had a soft side—one she kept very well hidden. He suppressed his smile at the idea of her being even remotely fluffy. 'All right. Explain.'

'The quick version: if I don't get married within the next six months, my grandfather's estate goes to my three half-brothers. Which he would emphatically not want to happen.'

'Then why make it a condition of his will?'

'I've asked myself that since the moment his solicitor gave me a copy of the will,' she said dryly. 'And I'm still coming up blank.'

He looked at her. 'I didn't have you down as the kind of person who was motivated by money.'

'I'm not. And I don't plan to cut the boys off with nothing.'

He waited, but she didn't elaborate about her brothers. He'd had no idea she even had any brothers. There were no family photographs on her desk: nothing personal at all, now he thought about it. 'Why did you ask *me* to marry you?' he asked.

'Because you have integrity,' she said.

Yes, he did. It was something he prided himself on. But Dominic was shocked to realise that her acknowledging that pleased him. It shouldn't bother him what she thought about him, good or bad. 'There are other people in the office who'd fit the bill,' he said. 'You said this was a business discussion.'

'It is.' She blew out a breath. 'The marriage needs to last for about a year, to give me time to sort out the estate properly and fairly.'

Which sounded to him as if she definitely wanted her brothers to get their share of the estate. His first instinct had been right: she wasn't the greedy sort.

'I'd also expect my husband to walk away at the end of that year,' she added, 'with a no-fault divorce, and no claim on the estate. Just as I'd have no claim on any of his assets.'

She was suggesting a marriage of convenience. Though the convenience was purely hers, he noted. 'What reason would your intended spouse have to marry you? Apart from being bowled over by your warmth and charm, of course,' he added.

Her eyes narrowed, and he knew he'd scored his point. He felt the tiniest bit guilty for sniping at her, but he knew she could give as good as she got. If anything, she could probably give better. Most of the lawyers he knew tried hard not to be on the end of one of Catriona's sharp looks or crisp words. She was the only person he'd ever met who could be scrupulously polite to someone while, at the same time, making it very clear she thought they were completely in the wrong. He'd been on the receiving end of some of those looks, himself.

'You want the partnership,' she said. 'Marry me for a year, and I'll step out of the running.'

Which was the equivalent of dropping the partnership in his lap.

And it was also incredibly insulting, because the implication was that she thought the partnership already had her name on it. He thought it might be a bit less clear-cut than that.

'So I'd marry you for your warmth, charm *and* your humility,' he said, making sure she could hear the slight edge to his voice.

She sat back in her seat and winced. 'I apologise. That didn't come across quite the way I intended it to.'

'You have a point.' Even if it annoyed him. 'You're my only competition, at this stage. If one of us steps down, the other will automatically get the partnership,' he said.

'Instead of it being you, me and briefcases at dawn,' she said lightly.

He'd get the partnership. The recognition of his hard work. The bonus would pay off his mother's mortgage and let him help his sisters out, too. Everything he wanted—everything he'd worked for—finally his. All he had to do in return was to be her husband for a year.

He was seriously tempted to say yes.

But this was Catriona Findlay. They'd rubbed each other up the wrong way since the very first case they'd worked on together, when they'd had opposite views on how the case should be run; in the end, she'd been right, and although she hadn't crowed about it he'd felt that she'd judged him.

He hated to admit it but she was one of the brightest people he'd ever met, so why hadn't she found a way round the terms of the will? There had to be more to this than simply needing a marriage on paper. He needed to know all the details, and think about what it meant for both of them, before he agreed.

He indicated her briefcase. 'I assume you've brought the will with you?'

She retrieved a large manila envelope from her briefcase and handed it to him. 'If you can find a loophole that means I don't have to marry, then I'd be grateful—because I can't find one.'

Catriona's attention to detail was legendary.

If she hadn't found a loophole, it was highly unlikely that he'd be able to see one. But Dominic looked anyway. And looked again. What he read was enough to make him ignore his favourite panini in the world—prosciutto, mozzarella, spinach and roasted red pepper with a smear of pesto—when their waitress brought it over.

'You're inheriting a castle in Scotland,' he said.

'Yes.'

Her expression said, *I've already told you that, so less of the dimwittery.*

He looked her squarely in the eye. 'And, since your grandfather's death—my condolences, by the way—you're a viscountess.'

At least this time she squirmed. 'Yes.'

'Do they know about this in the office?' Though he couldn't remember anyone mentioning her recent bereavement, let alone the fact that she now had a title. Catriona Findlay kept her cards so close to her chest that you couldn't even see the backs of them.

'It's not relevant to my job.'

That was a no, then. 'Technically,' he pointed out, 'I should be calling you "my lady".'

She rolled her eyes. 'We work for the same firm. You know perfectly well my name's Catriona. Or Ms Findlay, if you want to be formal.'

In other words, she wanted to be judged on her work, not her title. He liked that.

'And your youngest brother is called…' He stared at the will again. '*Finn* Findlay?'

'Half-brother,' she corrected. 'None of us has the same mother. And I'm pretty sure the rest of us are all very grateful that Finn's mother didn't get the chance to name any of us.'

'You'd make a wonderful Fifi,' he said blandly. 'Fifi Findlay.'

She said nothing.

'Fifi Froufrou Findlay,' he suggested—because that unruffled surface made him want to push her just that little bit further.

He saw the grin, the nanosecond before she masked it, and it took his breath away. He hadn't known that Catriona could smile like that, and he was glad he was sitting down because his knees had actually gone weak. Talk about hoist by his own petard. He'd meant to rattle her, but instead he'd succeeded in thoroughly rattling himself.

'Mitzi would've called you Ferrari. Or maybe Fergus,' Catriona said, equally blandly.

His own grin was barely suppressed—along with surprise that they shared the same sense of humour. He'd had no idea. It was a moment of pure joy—like an unexpected shaft of early morning winter sunlight turning a frost-covered lawn into a carpet of diamonds.

Then he switched to analysis mode as he ate his sandwich and read the document again. 'So you've got three half-brothers—all with different mothers, born five years apart.'

She rolled her eyes. 'It's pretty obvious that my father had a five-year itch. Fall in love, get bored, fall for someone else. There was another one after Finn's mother, but he died before he could marry her. He clearly made a bit more effort with my mother, because she lasted almost twice as long as the others.' She shrugged. 'Or maybe that was simply because she was the first.'

Dominic wasn't sure whether Catriona seemed more embarrassed or sad; and it sounded as if she wasn't close to any of her half-brothers. His own father had been just as selfish as hers seemed to be, putting his own needs before those of his family, but at least Dominic had been able to depend on the rest of his family and he was close to his sisters. It looked as if Catriona didn't have anyone.

'Why didn't your grandfather want the boys to inherit anything?' he asked.

There was a little pleat in the middle of her forehead, a tell-tale sign that she was concentrating. 'He thought they were growing up like my father, under the influence of their mothers. Feckless. He wanted the estate looked after properly and he was worried that they wouldn't do that.'

Whereas it was a given that Catriona would look after the estate properly without needing to be told. She was a perfectionist.

'Though I also don't think it's fair that I should get everything, and I intend to do something about that.' She frowned. 'But I can only do once the castle's on a sound financial footing.'

'That's reasonable—and realistic.' Which was a good combination, in Dominic's view. But it left her with a problem. One that would've made him as antsy as she looked, right now, were he in her shoes. 'You're right. There aren't any loopholes,' he said. 'You have to get married to inherit the castle. Does that affect the viscountcy?'

'No. Under Scots law, it goes to the firstborn, full stop. Which is me. For the record,' she added, 'if you married me, you wouldn't become Dominic Ferrars, Viscount of Linton. I'm afraid nobody would be calling you "Your Lordship".'

That comment was enough to make him want to don a kilt and kiss her stupid, until she begged him to—

No.

He dragged his mind back from that little scenario. Where the hell had that come from? Catriona was pretty, yes, but she was nothing like the women he dated. He didn't date that often, but he always made it very clear that any relationship was strictly for fun because he was concentrating on his career; he'd remained friends with most of his exes as well. Catriona Findlay wasn't the fun type.

The fact he could imagine kissing her, wasn't helpful.

At all.

'And the land isn't entailed?' he asked, trying to keep his mind completely on business and well away from the idea of how her mouth would feel against his.

'No. The land and title used to go together, but over time they've become separated. As I'm sure you're aware,' she said, 'entailments were made to help families ensure that the estate wasn't split up into smaller and smaller chunks with each generation, so the estate could support the holder of the title. But, if you had a dissolute child who was likely to gamble the entire estate on a game of cards, then the entail wasn't quite so helpful.'

Yeah. His father would definitely have gambled the whole lot on a game of cards, then made a hasty exit and left someone else to pick up the pieces. Just like he'd done to Dominic's mum.

'To break an entail, all you have to do is persuade the heir to agree to break it,' Dominic said, thinking out loud because Catriona obviously knew that, too. 'Did your father agree to do that?'

She shook her head. 'He didn't need to. Lark Hill's entail was broken more than a century ago. And I've been Gramps' heir since I was about five years old.'

'If you'd always known you'd inherit the castle—' and eventually become the Viscountess of Linton, after her grandfather's and her father's death, he reminded himself '—then why didn't you study estate management instead of law, or at the very least qualify in Scots law rather than English? Why are you working in London, not Glasgow or Edinburgh?'

'Because my father was still alive when I went to university, and Gramps could've altered his will at any time. I wanted to keep my options open rather than taking things for granted,' she said.

That sounded plausible. He wasn't going to quibble. 'Did your grandfather cut your father off completely?' he asked.

'No,' she said. 'Gramps left him money—just not the castle. Except, as my father died before Gramps did, that bequest went back into the estate.' She sighed. 'The castle needs a custodian who'll nurture it, update it and pass it on safely to the next generation. My father would've mortgaged Lark Hill to the hilt to buy an exclusive car.' Her eyes narrowed, betraying just how even the thought of it made her angry. 'Money that would be better spent on fixing the roof, battling the damp, installing a biomass boiler and developing the kind of amenities that attract paying visitors without causing ecological damage. Not to mention paying the inheritance tax.'

If spending the money carelessly was what her father would've done—and his own father would've seen it as a way of funding his gambling habit—then Dominic backed her grandfather's decision completely.

Catriona had been very specific about where the money needed to be spent, so she was clearly a realist and knew exactly what problems the estate faced. 'I think I understand the situation,' he said. 'What are your plans for the castle?'

'It needs a bit—no, a *lot*,' she corrected herself, 'of repair work. I need to sort that out, sell enough paintings to cover the inheritance tax, and then plan how I can make the estate support itself and generate an income for the boys.' She wrinkled her nose. 'Well, Tom's twenty-five and Lachy's twenty, so I suppose they should be classed as men. Finn's fifteen.'

At twenty and twenty-five, the two oldest half-brothers were surely capable of helping her. The fact she hadn't even suggested working with them to sort out the castle made him wonder what kind of men they were. Entitled and spoiled? Or they just hadn't reached her impossibly high standards yet? They were still young, so he wouldn't expect them to tackle the estate in the same way as she would; but surely they could've given her some kind of support? Had she turned them down, or had they not even offered in the first place? 'But?'

She spread her hands. 'They still need to find out who they are and what they want from life. And they make me feel as if I'm middle-aged, not thirty-five,' she admitted. 'Especially as, technically, I'm old enough to be Finn's mother.'

'Younger siblings have a habit of making you feel middle-aged,' he said wryly, thinking of his sisters.

'Yours, too?'

That rueful smile—it felt almost as if they were on the same side, instead of rivals, and that ruffled him. 'My sisters know who they are and what they want to do,' he said. 'But, yes, they've had their moments.' He looked at her. 'Are you going to leave the firm to manage the castle?'

'No. At least, not completely,' she said. 'I'll need to take a sabbatical until I've sorted things out.' She sighed. 'Which I think might take me a year.'

'Strictly speaking, then, you've already ruled yourself out of the partnership race,' he said. 'In which case, I could simply sit back and wait for it to drop into my lap.'

She spread her hands. 'If I don't marry, I won't inherit the castle and I won't need the sabbatical. Which will mean I'm very much still in the running for partner.'

'That might be a risk I'm prepared to take,' he drawled.

'It's always disappointing when you find out that your instincts about someone are wrong.' She reached over to take the manila envelope.

He held on to it. 'I didn't say I wouldn't help you.'

'You didn't say you would,' she countered.

'This needs a considered answer. I need time to think about it before I decide whether to agree or refuse,' he said.

She'd schooled her face into careful neutrality; he didn't have a clue what was going on in her head. Complicated didn't begin to describe her, and he wasn't sure whether that intrigued him or annoyed him more.

'How long do you need?' she asked.

He wanted to check out the differences between English and Scots law and really think about what this meant—for both of them. 'A day or so? And I might have some questions for you before then. Let's meet on Sunday morning to discuss it.'

'All right.' She paused. 'I'd better give you my mobile number, in case you want to send me any questions beforehand.' She took a business card from her briefcase and scribbled a number on the back.

He punched the number into his phone and texted her, keeping his face expressionless.

Yo, Fifi.

She glanced at the screen and this time there was a definite twitch at the corner of her mouth. A mouth, he suddenly realised, that was a perfect cupid's bow. How had he not noticed before that her lower lip was so full and lush? So kissable?

'Why, thank you, Fergus,' she said, batting her eyelashes at him, and it was all he could do not to laugh.

She checked her watch. 'I'd better head back. You know the drill: clients and paperwork. See you later. And thank you again.'

Then she was gone before he had a chance to say anything else.

Married.

For a year.

In name only.

And he'd be made partner.

The decision was his. Yes…or no?

CHAPTER TWO

Not a word. Not a single word.

By Saturday afternoon, Catriona was decidedly twitchy and glaring at her phone, willing it to make a sound.

If Dominic had any difficult questions, surely he would've contacted her with them by now? The fact he hadn't convinced her that tomorrow he was going to say no. In the meantime, he was clearly enjoying the power game by making her wait to hear from him.

Well, she wasn't playing.

She'd just picked up her phone, ready to call off their proposed meeting and tell him not to worry about it because she'd sort the situation out herself, when her phone pinged.

Meet you tomorrow morning outside Tower Hill Tube Station—Roman Wall side?

Technically, she could wait a while before texting back, to play him at his own game; but she knew that the waiting would annoy her just as much as it would annoy him. She'd rather make this as straightforward as possible.

Fine. 11?

Perfect. Wear something you can walk in. Weather forecast sunny, for once. Thought we could walk down the Thames path. See you by the Roman Wall.

Butterflies suddenly fluttered through her stomach, as if he'd just arranged a date with her, though she knew it was nothing of the kind. They would be discussing business: a marriage of convenience that would give them both what they wanted. So Catriona told herself not to be so ridiculous. But, even so, on Sunday morning she felt another of those odd little flutters in her stomach as she laced up her trainers and shrugged into her coat. Quivers that increased when she walked out of the Tube station and saw Dominic standing there; in walking boots, faded jeans and a fleece-lined rust-coloured jacket to keep out the late autumnal chill, he looked a lot more approachable than the shark-in-a-suit he was at work. His short dark hair was brushed back from his eyes, which were hidden from the bright November sun behind a pair of sunglasses; he looked like just another tourist taking a selfie next to the Roman Wall.

'It's only Roman up to the third layer of tiles, you know,' she said, walking up to him. 'Anything above that's medieval.'

'Says the woman who's heiress to a castle,' he said. 'A castle in Scotland, which repelled the Romans.'

'Look up the Antonine Wall,' she said dryly. 'And, just for your information, there's a Roman fort in Edinburgh.'

'I stand corrected,' he said, pushing up his sunglasses and looking her straight in the eye.

She wasn't sure if the glint in his brown eyes was teasing or a challenge, and it made her feel wrongfooted. 'I wasn't trying to score points. Gramps was a bit of a history nerd,' she said, wanting to explain. 'I inherited that gene.'

'Uh-huh.'

The question that had haunted her for days was mirrored in his expression: it made no sense that James Findlay, a man who cherished history, had put a clause in his will that would threaten the future of Lark Hill Castle. Why had he done it?

'As it's not raining, for once, let's go for that walk,' she said.

He gave her a little half-smile that made the fluttering in her stomach turn briefly into a tornado. 'Supplies, first.' He shepherded her over to the nearest coffee shop, bought them both coffee—and clearly he'd noticed how she drank her coffee, because he ordered exactly what she liked without needing to ask her, or suggesting that she might like one of the Christmassy options—and handed her a reusable cup.

'Thank you,' she said. 'The next coffees are on me.'

Dominic answered her with another of those unsettling smiles.

This time, her whole skin felt as if it was tingling.

How ridiculous. She didn't react to anyone like that, let alone her greatest rival. They'd never socialised outside work before, unless it was during some kind of team event: the sort of thing where she always found an excuse to leave early. And, although this wasn't a date, in a weird way it felt like it. Even more weirdly, she actually felt *shy* in his company. Shyness was something she hadn't experienced in years, and it made her antsy. She was used to knowing exactly what she was doing.

'Have you worked out yet why your grandfather made marriage a condition of you inheriting the castle?' he asked.

'No. Your guess would be as good as mine.'

'How? I didn't know him,' Dominic said.

'Precisely my point,' she said. 'The people who

did know him have no idea. The family solicitor doesn't know. Mrs MacFarlane—who's been our housekeeper ever since I can remember—doesn't know.'

'What about your half-brothers?'

'They weren't close to him or to my late grandmother. And that wasn't my grandparents' choice, before you ask,' she added. 'My father's next three wives weren't keen on traipsing up to Scotland from Cornwall, Sussex and Kent, respectively.'

'Does that mean you don't know them or their mothers very well, either?'

'The boys and I haven't spent much time together,' Catriona said. Once she'd been old enough to realise what both her parents were like, she'd made the effort to try and stay in touch with her half-brothers; but the boys' mothers had discouraged anything more than a birthday or Christmas card or gift. She'd just had to wait until they were old enough to rebel and contact her for themselves. But even then it wasn't like having a proper family. Not like the way her best friend's siblings teased her but absolutely had her back.

If they'd been a proper family, she would've talked to her half-brothers about the will in the certainty that they'd help her come up with a plan.

As things stood, she was on her own—and

she knew it. Which was why she was trying to recruit Dominic for her team.

'I'm not judging you,' Dominic said.

'Good.' Because she'd skewer him if he did. 'Did you have questions about the…' She could hardly call it a marriage. 'Business deal?' she amended.

'I've thought about it,' he said. 'And it doesn't sit well with me. Yes, I want the partnership—but I want it on the grounds that I'm the best one for the position.'

'If you're that concerned about it,' she said, 'you could always ask the partners the hypothetical question.' If Catriona hadn't backed out, would he still have been the one they'd chosen?

His eyes were hidden by the sunglasses he'd pushed back down again, but his irritation was clear in his voice. 'You're not helping your case.'

'I take it back,' she said, wincing. 'I didn't actually intend to insult you.' And, given what she was asking of him, he deserved some honesty from her. 'This whole inheritance thing has rattled me enough to make me unprofessional in the way I'm handling the situation. If I was the one choosing the new partner—your personality and smug mansplainer tendencies apart,' she added, just because honesty cut both ways, 'I'd pick you, because you have the edge over me when it comes to seeing the big picture.'

* * *

Dominic wasn't sure what had surprised him most: that Catriona had confessed to being all at sixes and sevens, that she thought he was the better candidate for the partnership, or that she'd zeroed in on his strengths and only made one searing comment—similar to the one he would've made about her, because he thought she was an ambitious, abrasive ball-breaker and he was glad his desk was the other side of their open-plan office from hers.

Her candour disarmed him enough to admit, 'Actually, I think I'd pick you because you have a better eye for the small details. Especially the ones that can flip a case on its head.'

Before she masked her expression, she looked as surprised as he'd felt.

They'd never actually complimented each other before.

Now he thought about it for the first time and realised that perhaps they complemented each other, too. With his strength being overall strategy and hers being a quick grasp of details, they could make a formidable team.

'Thank you for the compliment,' she said.

'You're welcome. And thank you for yours.' He took a swig of coffee, but it didn't do much to clear his head.

Could he and Catriona work together in some kind of partnership?

'If I agreed to do it,' he said, 'how would you see it working?'

'We'd have a quiet wedding, stay married for a year—at least until I've got things at Lark Hill running the way they need to be—and then apply for a quiet no-fault divorce,' she said. 'And we'd have a prenup.'

'You and I both know prenups aren't legally enforceable in the UK,' he said.

'But the courts will uphold one, provided we meet the conditions,' she reminded him. 'We both have independent legal representation; we both disclose full assets, liabilities and debts; there's no pressure, duress or misunderstanding to sign; it's fair; and the paperwork's drawn up properly and filed twenty-one days before the marriage.'

She'd listed every single condition without having to look them up—and she worked in corporate law, not family. This was a woman with a prodigious memory, never to be underestimated. 'I'm pretty sure that we can give a decent brief to our respective lawyers,' he said. 'All right. I'd be happy to sign a prenup. But what about your grandfather's lawyers? Will they consider that a marriage of convenience fulfils the conditions? Or do we have to convince them that it's real?'

'His lawyers,' she said, 'would probably advise a marriage of convenience as the best way forward. Gramps didn't actually specify that the marriage had to be real, so this is my only workable loophole.' She blew out a breath. 'On the other hand, I need to convince the boys the marriage is real, or they could challenge me—particularly if their mothers have something to say about it—which would mean an expensive legal case that neither the estate nor I can afford. I want Lark Hill to stay in the family and I want the castle to be a going concern.'

'So we're going to have to pretend the marriage is real?'

She gave a single, definite nod of her head. 'At least until they believe it.'

'What would convince them?'

'If we can prove that we know each other well,' she said. 'Which means we have to do some homework. Learn about each other. Ask questions. Make notes. Test each other until we're word-perfect on any answers.'

'Like that film my mum loves, where Andie MacDowell wants an apartment with a greenhouse, and Gerard Depardieu needs a green card—so, even though it's illegal, they help each other out,' he mused.

'My mother loves that film, too,' she said. 'It must be a nineties' idea of grand romance, though I don't think my mother actually married any of her husbands for a green card.' She shrugged. 'She's on her fifth divorce.'

It sounded as if Catriona had grown up without the kind of stability in her life that his mum had given him. If she'd had a new stepfather every few years, how did she get used to constant change? His own family had been in deep financial trouble, following his father's departure, but he and his sisters had always felt loved and wanted; whereas he thought that Catriona might be the archetypal 'poor little rich girl' who had plenty of money but whose family had no time for her.

A sudden tightness in her expression told him she'd realised that she'd told him more than she'd intended.

'If we're echoing the film: I inherit my castle, the way Andie MacDowell gets her dream apartment; and you get your partnership rather than Depardieu's green card,' she said. 'Though what I'm asking you for isn't illegal, and you don't need to be married to get the partnership.'

'Marrying you takes out the competition for the partnership. Plus, it has the bonus of making you indebted to me,' he said.

She wrinkled her nose. 'That's not who you are.'

'It also feeds my knight on a white charger complex.'

This time, she laughed. 'You don't have one of those, either.'

Interesting. She didn't think he wanted to feel superior or desperately needed. 'So who do you think I am?' he asked, genuinely wanting to know the answer.

'A workaholic who wants to prove himself,' she said. 'Ambitious. I think what you want is public recognition of your talent and the fact you've got there by sheer hard work, not by family connections or the old boys' network.'

Which was right on the money. Scarily so. He'd never met anyone before who'd really understood who he was, deep down. He wasn't sure whether the fact that Catriona seemed to have worked it out—and so fast—was more worrying or intriguing.

'Though,' she said, 'I've always wondered why you do so much *pro bono* work.'

'It balances out the corporate shark stuff,' he said. He wasn't going to tell her the real reason. 'Aren't you going to ask me what I think of you?'

She shrugged. 'An ambitious workaholic: much like you.'

One who didn't use family connections either, he thought.

'Ambition is probably why we've always rubbed each other up the wrong way at work,' she added.

'Maybe. But I think you hide behind the image

of being a scary ball-breaker,' he said. 'I'd like to know what's behind that image.'

'My image,' she said, 'is like the hoardings you see round the scaffolding of ancient tourist attractions in Italy. Painted with exactly what's underneath it, or what will be underneath it once the cracks are fixed. The tourist attractions, I mean; I don't have any cracks and I don't need fixing.'

He didn't believe her.

He wanted to know what was really underneath her painted hoardings.

Though he knew that a bulldozer approach wasn't going to work. He'd be better off trying something more oblique. 'You said you wanted to give your half-brothers a share of the estate but without selling any land. Tell me about the castle,' he said instead.

'Currently, it's supported by tenant rents and some investment income. Until I've scrutinised the figures properly, I can't tell if the investments are good enough, though I suspect they're probably not or Gramps would've sorted out the roof and the boiler before now,' she said. 'I'm absolutely not going to put up the tenants' rents, so I'll need to look at the castle itself and work out how it can make money.'

'Guest accommodation? Hosting weddings?' he suggested.

'You could be describing practically every castle in Scotland,' she said dryly. 'Not to mention all the stately homes in England. Lark Hill needs to offer something different. Something to make the castle stand out—and make enough money to support the estate.' She paused. 'What do you think of when you think of Scotland?'

'Tartan,' he said. 'Do you have your own tartan?'

'I'm ignoring that,' she said, narrowing her eyes at him.

'All right. Scotland to me is kilts, Loch Ness, mountains and Highland dancing—the stuff over swords. Oh, and bagpipes.'

'Keep going,' she said, and he wondered how much of this her steel-trap mind was remembering.

'Whisky. Heather. Honey. Porridge. Salmon.' He thought a bit more. 'Grouse. Haggis. Cattle with big horns. Will that do?'

She nodded. 'For starters, I'm ignoring kilts. We're on the coast, so it's no to a loch and absolutely no to fictitious monsters. The castle's on a hill rather than a mountain, as you might have guessed from the name. We're not in the Highlands, and dancing won't bring in enough money; and it's a no to bagpipes as well.'

She was demolishing everything he suggested, he noticed. Not even questioning or considering any of it. And that annoyed him. If she wanted to work as a team, then why wasn't she treating him as her equal?

'Whisky—we don't have a still. There's no heather on the hill; very probably no to honey—to the best of my knowledge, we don't have bees on the estate; and, although some of the tenants have arable land and probably grow oats, I don't know whether the quantities would work for commercial production of Lark Hill brand porridge, granola or oatcakes. No river, so it's a no to salmon. Grouse—even if we do have them, that's an absolute no to shooting. I'll ignore haggis. Some of the tenants have cattle, but I'm not sure whether or not they're Highland cows.'

'Is this a game where you shoot down every single thing I say?' he asked, damping down the fact he was impressed by how she'd retained everything he'd said—*and* in order.

'No,' she said, though he noticed she didn't remark on how harshly she'd come across or how it might have made him feel. Today, it was as if she didn't have any emotions; there was no trace of the sense of humour and wicked grin that had captivated him in their lunch meeting.

'Your non-Scots point of view is useful, actually,' she added. 'It helps me think and sort out what's viable.'

Did she consider herself to be Scots, even though she had a very English accent? Interesting. He thought a bit more. 'My sisters love *Outlander*.'

'We're not *quite* going to be able to offer our guests time travel, even if we could offer historical dress and traditional dinners,' she said wryly. 'And, again, the books were meant to be set in the Highlands.'

'Much further north than you. Got it. Given that you're on the coast, how about islands?'

'There are islands around Edinburgh,' she said, 'but they're mostly uninhabited, and none of them belong to Lark Hill.'

'Shortbread?' He gave her a sidelong look. 'In a tartan tin.'

She narrowed her eyes at him. 'Basically, what you're telling me is that when you think of Scotland, it's tartan, food and scenery.'

'Yup.' He loved the way she'd chopped up his list and categorised it so swiftly. 'So what's the castle like?'

'A lot of the rooms are shut off, with the furniture covered in dust sheets, so they don't have to be heated,' she said. 'At the moment, "shabby chic" is probably the best way to describe it.'

But something in her expression told him that it meant something more to her than that. And her very stubbornness in wanting to save the castle, despite it being a huge challenge, tempted him to join her. Be a team with her.

A team.

Despite his earlier reservations, he was pretty sure it could work. They were very different people—but combining their strengths would make them a formidable pair. Besides, if he agreed to help her he'd get the partnership: and then he'd need to find himself a new challenge.

Saving the castle with her might be just what he needed.

And he wasn't going to listen to the little voice in his head that was pointing out it wasn't just the business side of things that attracted him: it was Catriona herself.

Not relevant.

Not true.

He'd push her a bit further, first. Find out if she would work with him. And then he'd accept her offer. 'Let's try brainstorming this the other way round,' he said. 'Tell me what Lark Hill means to you.'

Home.

It was the only place Catriona had felt settled, as a child. The only place she'd felt wanted.

Not that she was going to admit that to Dominic.

Even if she sold her flat in Primrose Hill and paid off the mortgage, she knew that any capital raised plus her savings wouldn't last long in propping up the castle. The estate needed to change so it could support itself.

And Dominic was waiting for an answer.

'History,' she said. 'It's been in my family for centuries.'

'From what you've told me, the building will need a major overhaul to make it suitable for visitors,' he said. 'On the physical asset side, you have the castle, its lands and its tenants.'

'I'm not fleecing my tenants by putting up their rent,' she said again. 'Gramps always said that with rights came responsibility. I agree with him.'

'That brings us back to the castle and its lands,' he said. 'Which means you need to look at using either the buildings or the land to make money. The history angle could be useful. On balance, we're looking at tourism or production.'

We.

Did that mean Dominic saw them as a team?

Catriona had never considered being a team with him, before. But that was what she was asking him to do, wasn't it? If he married her, they'd be Team Domiona, or maybe Team Catrinic. Neither sounded right, to her ears.

Team Fifi-Fergus.

She shook herself. Now that was *really* ridiculous.

Of course they weren't a team.

But they could be.

The idea made her feel warm all over; it shocked her that she was even considering it, but maybe she and Dominic could be a partnership. His grasp of the big picture and her grasp of details would work well together. They'd dovetail. They'd probably—no, *definitely*—argue, but they'd dovetail.

'There are a lot of things we could do with the building. A hotel or holiday apartments and a restaurant—which, as you say, lots of other Scottish castles and stately homes can offer. But we could offer organic food grown locally, either by the castle itself or by the tenants,' he said. 'A shop showcasing local craftspeople and local produce. An education centre, even, if there's something specific to the site—flora, fauna or something big historically.'

'That's the tourism side,' she said. 'And you mentioned production. There are outbuildings.'

'Which gives us options. They could be fitted out as accommodation; or, if we went the production route, either as workplaces or sales outlets.'

'Production.' She thought about it. 'You see Scotland in terms of food. If the tenants grow enough oats, maybe Lark Hill oatcakes?'

'And is there something special about the oats?' he asked. 'You need a niche to differentiate yourself. Gluten-free, maybe? Or something else—my youngest sister has eczema and she swears by oat-based toiletries.'

'I like that idea,' she said. 'We could make shampoo, cleanser and moisturiser in bars and wrap them in compostable packaging rather than put them in plastic pots. Provided we have the raw materials and the figures stack up.'

'Sustainable's a good way to differentiate Lark Hill,' he said. 'If we produced food-based items, we could use compostable packaging, too. Or drink. If there's space for a still in the cellars, we could consider small-batch production. Lark Hill special malt.'

'Can you actually make whisky from oats?' she asked.

'I have no idea. In America they use rye. So I guess you could use another grain.'

'Though, even if we had the right grains to make whisky, we'd need an expert to make it for us. Not to mention the cost of a still and whatever else you need to make the whisky, getting a licence, and how long the whisky would need to be aged,' she said. 'It'd be years before we could start selling it, let alone pay off the cost of production.'

'So that's another no?'

'It'll stay on the list of potential options,' she corrected, 'but it'll be a long-term project rather than a short-term one.'

He looked at her. 'All right, Your Ladyship.' At her narrowed eyes, he smiled. 'I think you've answered all my questions. I accept your proposal.'

CHAPTER THREE

Dominic had agreed to marry her.

Catriona wasn't sure whether that was relief or fear flooding through her veins. Maybe a weird mixture of both. 'Thank you,' she said.

'When do we need to do the deed?' He did a quick internet search on his phone. 'If we want to get married in less than a week, we'd have to go to America.'

'But we also need to have the prenups done twenty-one days before the wedding,' she reminded him. 'That'll take three or four days to sort out anyway, so we might as well give the twenty-nine days' notice to marry in England.'

He nodded agreement. 'When we give notice, we need to name the venue.' He paused. 'Do you want to get married at Lark Hill?'

Catriona had to remind herself to breathe.

She'd once thought to get married at Lark Hill. When she'd been younger and foolish, and fallen in love with her personal trainer at the gym. She'd thought that Luke loved her back and had secretly dreamed about a winter wedding at the chapel in the castle grounds. She'd be wearing a lacy cream dress topped with dark green velvet cloak, to go with the Findlay tartan, and a crown of cream rosebuds in her hair; she'd carry a bouquet of cream roses and heather. Luke would be wearing a kilt with a Prince Charlie jacket and a rose prettied up with heather in his buttonhole. Her grandfather would walk her down the aisle, something romantic would be played on a harp, and it would be snowing outside…

Except she'd discovered that Luke had the same flaw as her parents: the same inability to be faithful. When she looked back, the signs had been there right from the start; but she'd so wanted to believe that she was wrong and love really did exist that she'd ignored them.

Then she'd been forced to face the truth. Luke had claimed that she was cold and he'd needed to find warmth elsewhere; but if he'd really loved her surely he would've taught her to be warmer? Anyway, being reserved wasn't the same thing as being cold. But the experience had made her vow never to get involved with anyone again. And she'd stopped believing in love.

'The castle isn't licensed for weddings,' she said. The chapel was a different matter; but it felt wrong to have the kind of wedding where you walked down the aisle when it wasn't for real. 'I think it'd be best if we had a register office ceremony. The nearest one to the office, so we can get married at lunchtime and be back at work in the afternoon,' she said.

'A wedding like that wouldn't convince my sisters—or my mum,' Dominic said. 'I don't think it's likely that'd convince your mum or your half-brothers, either.'

'It doesn't matter what my mother thinks,' Catriona said. 'She'll be too busy to attend the wedding, in any case.'

'But it matters what the mothers of your half-brothers think—and your half-brothers themselves,' he pointed out. 'Otherwise, as you said, they could contest the will.'

Dominic was absolutely right, and it irritated her. 'I don't want a massive wedding. I'm definitely not going to do the fussy dress and veil and flowers bit. That isn't me.' She squashed down the memories of the wedding she'd once wanted. At least this one—ironically, as it was a fake—would be honest. 'The whole point is to have a quiet, understated wedding.'

'Like the quiet, understated shark-in-a-suit lawyer you are?'

'That,' she said coolly, 'is exactly how I'd describe you.'

'Just as well our children will never ask me how you proposed to me,' he drawled.

That stung. Which was crazy, because she didn't want children. She didn't want to fail a child, the way her parents had failed her. And she absolutely wasn't planning to have a baby with Dominic Ferrars. 'I used the right language. Four little words,' she reminded him stiffly.

'But you didn't go down on one knee.'

Did he really think she wasn't going to rise to a challenge like that? Well, then. Let him learn not to underestimate her in future. She dropped to one knee, batted her eyelashes at him and held up her hands in supplication, ignoring the tourists who'd stopped in a little crowd to watch them. 'Dominic Ferrars, I know you've already said yes—but, as you want it the traditional way, will you marry me?'

'Go on, my son! Say yes!' someone catcalled.

They both ignored the crowd, and Dominic hauled her back to her feet. 'Point taken, Your Ladyship,' he said coolly.

'Catriona,' she reminded him.

'Catriona.' He folded his arms and stared at her.

The crowd, denied of the smooch and the declaration of love they'd expected, grumbled and moved on.

And Catriona felt as if she'd lost the point rather than scored it.

'Let's walk,' he said.

'Sure.' Though walking didn't settle her thoughts,

the way it usually did. And, despite the sunshine, it was chilly enough for her to wish she'd brought gloves. Had she made a mistake in asking Dominic to marry her? Or had this been her grandfather's way of saying that he knew Lark Hill would be a total millstone round her neck, and the only way he could stop her being dragged down by it was by putting that ridiculous clause in the will, so she could refuse to inherit the castle and at the same time keep her conscience clear?

The more she thought about it, the more muddled it became.

'What if you fall in love with someone, the day after you marry me?' Dominic asked, breaking into her thoughts.

She scoffed. 'That'd be highly unlikely.' How could she fall in love, when she knew first-hand that love didn't exist? Though she didn't want to argue that particular point. 'But, if I do and if he's worth waiting for, then he'll think I'm worth waiting for, too,' she said. She looked at him. 'What if *you* fall in love with someone, the day after you marry me?'

'That'd be highly unlikely for me, too; but your answer works for me,' he said.

Why was it so unlikely that he'd fall in love—or that someone would fall for him? When she looked at it objectively, Dominic Ferrars was easy on the eye. More than easy, with those soft brown eyes, those gorgeous cheekbones and that beautiful mouth. And he might not irritate other women in the same way that he irritated her.

And that was another point. One that needed addressing, if they were going to make this work. 'We need to convince people that the reason we've never got on before is because we're so similar. But then, when we realised those similarities are things we have in common, we spent more time together and eventually fell for each other, so we got married.'

'That might convince your side,' he said, 'but it won't convince mine.'

'Do we need to convince yours?'

'If we want yours to stay convinced, then probably,' he said.

'Your family will want to come to the wedding?' She shook her head. 'I'm not good enough at acting to carry that off. I want a small, quick legal ceremony, not a huge fuss.'

'Why are you so against weddings?' Dominic paused, as if thinking about it, then answered his own question. 'You said your dad was married four times,' he said. 'And your mum's on her fifth divorce. I guess that'd make anyone twitchy about weddings.'

Not to mention her failed engagement, but Dominic didn't need to know about that. She nodded, but said nothing, glad that he wasn't going to push her further.

'Then our cover story should be that you want to marry me, but you don't want a fuss since your parents have already cornered the wedding market.'

'We could take a half day, change into something that looks vaguely wedding-like for the register office, and it'll be just you and me—and two witnesses we borrow from the street,' she said. 'If that works for you. Though, before this goes too far, don't you want to get married properly—I mean, to someone you love and who loves you back?'

For someone who clearly didn't believe in love, Dominic thought, it was surprising that she'd asked. 'No,' he said. 'Marriage isn't in my game plan.' He'd done his share of responsibility and bringing up a family when his sisters were small. With his mother working several jobs to keep their family afloat, he'd learned to do housework and to cook, and he'd got a paper round as soon as he could. His mum had refused to let him contribute to the housekeeping, but she couldn't stop him buying her a bunch of cheap flowers and chocolates for the girls after he'd been paid on a Sunday morning.

In sixth form, he'd had a part-time job in the local coffee shop at weekends, and had done two evenings a week washing up in the local pub kitchen; during his university years, he'd lived at home to save costs and swapped his kitchen job for working behind the bar three evenings a week as well as being an intern in a local solicitor's during university holidays. He'd landed his training contract through hard work and grit rather than family connections, and after he'd qualified as a solicitor he'd spent one last year at home to make sure both his sisters were on the way to being settled.

Only then had he gone to London and allowed himself to climb the ladder. His aim was to be able to support his family and make sure he was their safety net—that they'd never have to live under the shadow of debt, ever again. When he'd met Catriona, he'd had her measure from the start: ambitious and privileged. Although now he was beginning to realise that might be what she wanted people to think, and underneath that layer of privilege was a very different person.

'A marriage of convenience works for me,' he said.

'OK. So we get married, and then maybe… maybe you come to Scotland with me? And, after a week's "honeymoon" at the castle—' she actually did the finger quotes, as if to make it clear to Dominic that she meant nothing of the kind '—you come back to London and I stay at Lark Hill.'

'And then what?'

She shrugged. 'You get the partnership, I sort out the castle, and we divorce in a year's time.'

'For a details woman, you've missed out something fairly crucial,' he said.

'What?'

'Your family,' he said. 'When are you going to announce the marriage?'

'When we're at Lark Hill,' she said.

'How? Are you going to call them?'

She shook her head. 'I'll send them a text,' she said. 'Or maybe an email.'

'My sisters,' he said, 'would be up in arms if I did that. As would my mother.'

'And your father?' she asked.

Of course she'd notice what he'd quietly left out. 'I don't have any contact with my father,' he admitted.

'Why?'

He decided to answer a question with a question. 'Would you have much contact with yours, if he'd still been alive?'

'Only insofar as I'm the heir to Lark Hill. The one who might have a bit of influence over the purse strings,' she said dryly.

'There's your answer,' he said.

She blinked. 'Was your dad like mine, then?'

'Absent, for most of my life,' Dominic said. 'I haven't seen him since my mum was pregnant with my youngest sister. That was when he walked out on us, for someone else.' Leaving his debts behind him, though Catriona didn't need to know that. Or how bad those debts had been.

'I'm sorry,' she said.

'Not your fault,' he said.

'Did your mum ever remarry?'

'No,' he said. 'Though she's been seeing someone for the last three years. The girls and I think he's perfect for her, but…' He spread his hands. 'Let's say my father left her with a few trust issues.'

'It sounds as if you and I have similar issues,' she said. 'A dad who did whatever he wanted, whenever he wanted—and who left us when we were small.'

Except Dominic had a mother, two sisters and an extended family who loved him. It sounded as if the only people Catriona had been close to had been her grandparents—neither of whom was still alive.

How hard her grandfather's funeral must've been: saying goodbye to the last person she'd been close to.

And it couldn't be easy for her now. She was taking over as the viscountess, shouldering the management of the castle and its estate, and having to step back from a job she loved. Although he suspected Catriona might have originally been offered her job at the firm through family connections, he couldn't fault her work ethic. She put in the same kind of hours that he did and she was good at her job.

He curbed the impulse to take her hand, because he was pretty sure she'd hate that. She wasn't the demonstrative kind at work. If you needed a hug, Catriona Findlay wasn't the go-to person. She was completely self-sufficient and made it clear that she expected everyone else around her to respect that.

Though now Dominic had a much better idea of what had made her so self-sufficient in the first place; and he rather thought that her painted hoardings had a few layers beneath them, despite her protests.

The silence between them was easy rather than awkward as they walked along the Thames path. When they reached Embankment and he judged that she had her equilibrium back, he said, 'Want to break for lunch and make a list?'

'Sure. My bill.'

'You paid for lunch on Friday,' he pointed out.

'And you paid for coffee this morning.'

'We're not keeping score, Catriona,' he said gently.

'You're doing me a huge favour,' she reminded him.

Not just for her; their deal would help him

achieve everything he'd spent years working for. 'If I'd been the one who needed to get married for inheritance reasons, would you have accepted my proposal?' he asked.

She wrinkled her nose. 'I would've needed time to think about it. And I would've had questions.'

'You've given me time and answers. I've thought about it and my answer's yes. So lighten up a little,' he said.

'Sorry. I'm not good at…' She flapped a hand.

'Doing the fluffy stuff?' he suggested.

She gave him a wry nod.

'I think,' he said, 'we both might need some carbs. And there's a pub not far from here that does the most amazing macaroni cheese.'

'Sounds great.' She gave him a dazzling smile.

At the pub, she waved away the menu. 'I'll take your recommendation,' she said.

'Glass of wine?' Dominic asked.

'Whatever you're having,' she said.

Glad that she wasn't a wine bore, he ordered them both the macaroni and a glass of chianti.

'While we're waiting for the food, we might as well make a start on the getting-to-know-each-other dossiers,' he said. 'Let's start with family. Your grandfather was James Findlay, and your grandmother was…?'

'Morag.'

He made a note. 'Your father was Thomas, an only child who died ten years ago; your mother is…?'

'Victoria.'

He didn't ask if Catriona's mum had been named after the queen or if Catriona was related to the English royal family; he knew her response would be arctic and that wouldn't be helpful. 'Aunts and uncles?' he asked instead.

'No,' she said. 'My father was an only child. My mother fell out with her family when she married him, and never really made it up with them after the divorce.'

'Why? Because they didn't think the son of a viscount was good enough for her?' They certainly wouldn't approve of *him*, then. Dominic thought. His background was much more modest.

'I doubt it. More that my mother does things her way.' Catriona shrugged. 'Yes, I could've got in touch with them when I was older. But I had better things to do with my time than chasing after people who clearly weren't interested in me.'

That sounded as if Catriona had been hurt by their abandonment, at least when she was younger, but her expression said very clearly that she wasn't going to discuss it. Instead, he asked, 'What does your mother do?'

'Marries people,' she said.

Clearly his surprise showed in his face, because she sighed. 'My mother doesn't actually have a job. She lives off a combination of divorce settlements and a trust fund. She likes yachts, parties, Ascot, that sort of thing.'

The way she said it made it sound as if Catriona didn't like any of that. And he had the distinct feeling that she didn't like talking about her mother, either. 'OK. Your half-brothers. Tell me about them.'

'Tom surfs, Lachy's into his computers, but hasn't bothered with university and doesn't have a job at the moment either, and Finn…' She shook her head. 'Finn's your average stroppy, testosterone-fuelled teen. And their mums all come from society backgrounds, so they don't have to worry about money.'

He could see why the idea of the estate being in their control worried her. Being so young, they wouldn't have enough life experience or maturity to shoulder the burden of running the castle. 'Anything else?'

She spread her hands. 'We're simply not a close family. Clearly yours is different. Perhaps I could trouble you for the same information.'

She made it sound as if this was a business brief, instead of telling her about the people he loved. And this had the potential to be a deal-breaker. 'My grandparents died a few years ago.

My father isn't part of my life and didn't have any brothers or sisters. My mum's called Ginny, and she's a manager at a supermarket.' He lifted his chin. This was the point where he might decide not to help Catriona, after all, depending on her reaction. 'When I was growing up, Mum worked several part-time jobs. Cleaning the school first thing, being a domestic cleaner in the morning and afternoon, doing a shift as a school dinner lady at lunchtime, and doing a shift stacking shelves in the supermarket in the evening.'

'That's a tough schedule. I can see where you get your work ethic,' she said, and Dominic realised he'd half-expected Catriona, as a viscountess, to be scathing of his background.

But there was no judgement in her face, no scorn or censure; whereas he'd judged her, and got it badly wrong. Catriona's family might be snobs, but she wasn't.

'My middle sister Tilly's thirty-one,' he said, 'and she's currently on maternity leave with her son. She's an office manager. Suzy, the baby of the family, is twenty-eight; she's a personal trainer.'

Was it his imagination, or did Catriona just flinch? Why would the idea of a personal trainer make her lose her equilibrium? He filed that one away for later.

'And you're close to them?' she asked.

'We have a family Zoom call at eight o'clock every Wednesday night, without fail. Except for the night that Tilly was in labour, when we thought it was only fair to let her off.' Catriona let out a soft chuckle at that, and he continued, 'And we were all waiting for Joe to ring us and tell us the second she had the baby. Plus, Birmingham's an easy drive or train journey at the weekend. I go home for my mum's Sunday lunch once a month. And they all know they can come and stay with me, any time they like.'

'You don't have much of an accent,' she observed.

'I've lived in London for a long time now, so it's softened. But it comes out a bit stronger when I visit home.' He smiled at her, then asked, 'When was the last time you saw your mum or your b— half-brothers?' he corrected himself swiftly.

'My mother…' She thought about it. 'I guess sometime in the spring. The boys were at Gramps's funeral, a couple of weeks ago.'

Obviously her mum hadn't been there. He winced. 'Sorry. Tactless.'

She shrugged. 'I already told you we weren't close. By the way, you've missed out aunts and uncles. As you know, I don't have any.'

'My mum has three older sisters. They get together once a month—funnily enough, it's usually the same weekend I go home. Sunday lunch tends to be a barbecue in the summer,' he said. 'At Christmas, they take turns hosting. It's a bit of squash, with all the kids sitting on folding garden chairs at a pasting table, and everyone brings something as a contribution towards dinner.' Just thinking of his family made him smile, remembering all the warmth and the shared laughter. Catriona didn't have that, which he imagined must make her feel pretty lonely.

'Sounds fun,' Catriona said lightly, and gave him her best smile, hoping he wouldn't see the wistfulness underneath. What would it to be like, to be part of a big extended family?

Her own Christmases had always been spent at Lark Hill. And they'd always been small-scale, just the three of them, her and her grandparents, and occasionally Mrs MacFarlane—the housekeeper—rattling around in the castle. The turkey that lasted for days, until they were all utterly sick of turkey sandwiches, turkey salad, turkey fricassee and turkey soup. Her dad was never there for Christmas because he always had a new family to attend to, her half-brothers were busy with their own families and she was never invited there anyway, and her mum always preferred to spend Christmas with friends in Monaco, Hawaii, or somewhere else where children were surplus to requirements.

Even though Catriona was no longer a child, she still didn't fit in with her mother's lifestyle.

'We play charades and board games,' Dominic continued, 'take assorted dogs for a quick walk and get back in time to have pudding watching the King's Speech. The usual family stuff. Uncle Glenn's homemade wine is a rite of passage, and Uncle Bill brings his guitar. His band plays the local pub circuit, so he's the one who gets us all singing, whether it's carols or Christmas pop songs—and he always makes my mum and her sisters sing "All I Want for Christmas is You", wearing fluffy Santa hats. Nobody cares that everyone is slightly out of tune because they're too busy enjoying themselves.' He looked at her. 'You?'

'Me?'

'Christmas traditions,' he said. 'You must have some.'

None—and she didn't want him to pity her. Time for a diversion. 'It's Hogmanay all the way in Scotland rather than Christmas. First footing, "Auld Lang Syne" and fireworks.' They'd always done the first footing and sung the song, though she'd watched other people's fireworks from her bedroom in the turret rather than enjoying them close up. Mrs MacFarlane had bought sparklers, a couple of times, but that was about it. Hopefully Dominic wouldn't press her for details until she was ready to admit just how quiet the holiday season always was for her.

'Right.' He made a note. 'What did you want to be, when you were small?'

Loved.

She pushed the thought away. 'The usual,' she drawled. 'A doctor or a lawyer. You?'

'A trapeze artist,' he said.

She shook her head, surprised. It was the last thing she'd expected, and it intrigued her. 'Why a trapeze artist?'

'One of the people Mum used to clean for gave us tickets to the circus when I was about eight. I was spellbound,' he explained. 'It wasn't one of the circuses with animals—I would've wanted to set them all free—but a people one, with clowns and acrobats and fire-jugglers.'

'I've never been to a circus,' she said.

'I haven't, for years,' he said. 'But that high-wire act made me think about the world and what was out there.'

'Have you ever done one of those circus skills courses?' she asked.

He smiled. 'I've thought about it, but things get in the way. You know how it is.'

Work. Yeah. Though in other ways she was grateful that work took up all her time. It meant she didn't have time to get close to other people and be let down again. 'What made you decide to become a lawyer?' she asked.

'I wanted to do something that would make a difference,' he said. 'Plus, I knew it'd pay enough to help me support my mum and my sisters.' He paused. 'You?'

'One of my teachers suggested it. And it was a good fit,' she said.

'Did you go to school at Lark Hill?'

'No. I was a day pupil in London until I was about seven,' she said. 'Then I went to boarding school.'

'You went to boarding school at the age of *seven*?' He sounded shocked.

'My parents both went to boarding school.' She shrugged. 'It was a given that I'd do the same.' Just her time there had started when she'd been a few years earlier than they had.

'But didn't you—well, miss your family?'

If hers had been close, the way his sounded, she would've hated being torn away from them to go to school. But her family wasn't close. Boarding had taught her to be self-sufficient, and the bullying had given her a thick skin. 'It was OK,' she said. 'And I went to Lark Hill in the holidays.'

'So you lived with your grandparents rather than with your mum?'

'During the holidays. And I was lucky. Some

of the international students didn't get to go home until the summer holidays.'

'OK.' He blew out a breath. 'Sorry. It's not my place to judge.'

'It is what it is,' she said. 'You get used to it.'

'I didn't mean to drag up difficult memories.'

'You didn't. It's fine.' But her smile felt over-bright, and she could see in his eyes that he could tell.

The macaroni cheese saved her from having to talk for a bit, but in a way that was a bad move because it gave her room to think. To realise how different their upbringings had been. Dominic's family had clearly struggled financially, but it sounded as if he was really close to his mum and his sisters. Catriona had never wanted for anything money could buy; but, with parents who regarded her as something that curtailed their fun and grandparents who were firmly part of the stiff-upper-lip brigade, she'd never really felt loved.

Which was probably why she'd fallen so hard for Luke. He'd given her everything she'd thought she wanted.

Except it had all been for show. And she'd found out the hard way that Luke had been in love with the idea of dating the granddaughter of a viscount rather than in love with her. With the idea of marrying into money. And he'd had the nerve to call *her* cold?

'Pudding?' Dominic asked, when they'd finished the pasta.

'Just coffee, please,' she said.

He ordered two coffees when the waitress cleared their places, then looked at her. 'Right. We've done family, and sort of education. What were your A levels?'

'English, history and economics,' she said.

'Same as mine, so that's easy to remember.' He gave her a wry smile. 'And I'd guess yours were all top grades.'

She nodded. 'Same for you?'

'Yes.' He paused. 'Then obviously you took a law degree. Where did you go?'

'Brasenose. Oxford,' she clarified. 'You?'

'Birmingham.'

He'd said his family lived in Birmingham, she remembered. 'Did you live at home rather than going away to uni?'

'It worked out for the best,' he said.

It sounded as if he'd stayed at home to lessen the financial burden on his family. She respected that. 'And you did your Legal Practice course and training there, too?'

'Yes. And I assume you did all yours in London?'

'Yes.' He didn't need to know that she'd done her training at a different firm. Ashamed of how badly she'd been taken in by Luke and what a fool she'd made of herself, she'd moved on as soon as she could after she'd split up with Luke and had lost contact with everyone at her old firm. 'What do you do when you're not at work?'

He raised an eyebrow. 'According to my family, I just work. Which I'm guessing is the same for you.'

'I read historical novels. Historical non-fiction, too.'

'Crime for me,' he said. 'Not the gory stuff—I like the clever ones with puzzles to solve.' He smiled. 'I go to the gym after work to clear my head. Suzy's designed me a tailor-made HIIT programme so I don't get bored.'

Luke had designed her a tailor-made programme, too. If only she'd kept their relationship purely business instead of being stupid enough to fall for a charmer who'd turned out to be as much of a cheat as her father. 'I'd rather walk in the park,' she muttered.

'Even on wet days?'

She looked away. 'Yes.'

'So you like fresh air and green spaces. Got it,' he said. 'I won't ask you to join me in the gym. Though it might be fun to spar with you.'

'Spar?'

'Boxing,' he said. 'It's great for clearing your head after a rubbish day. Ten punches, ten burpees, ten star jumps, rinse and repeat. By the time you're sweating, you're ready to conquer the world again.'

'I'll take your word for it,' she said.

'Anything else apart from reading? Music? Cinema?'

'I sometimes listen to the radio.'

'What sort of music?'

'Classical. And I might go to the theatre if there's something special on.' She paused. 'You?'

'I'll go and see any band with a decent guitarist,' he said. 'Probably Uncle Bill's influence. He did try teaching me, but I was never good enough to be in a band. Though he also taught me how to appreciate good guitar playing. Blues, rock, a bit of folk.'

That surprised her enough to look at him. 'You like going to see music?' It was a side to him she'd never expected.

'There's nothing like being in a crowd, all singing along with the band to your favourite songs,' he said.

'It's not something I've ever really done,' she said.

He batted his eyelashes at her. 'And there was I waiting for you to tell me that you're a bagpipes virtuoso. How disappointing of you, Fifi.'

She couldn't help smiling. His sense of the absurd was infectious. Why had she never really noticed before that he had this dry, whimsical streak? 'Apart from the fact I can't play them, I'm pretty sure you wouldn't enjoy virtuoso bagpipes, my dear Fergus.'

'I'm prepared to give it a go,' he said. 'Actually, I love Celtic folk-rock. How far is Lark Hill from Edinburgh?'

'Half an hour or so—obviously depending on the traffic,' she said.

'Then I'll find us a band to see on our honeymoon,' he said.

Honeymoon.

Was he expecting a real honeymoon? One with hand-holding and smooching and…? Catriona wasn't sure what terrified her more: the fact that she could actually imagine holding Dominic's hand and smooching with him, or the fact that a deeply buried part of her actually liked the idea of doing it.

This wasn't supposed to happen. This was a business deal, not an emotional one.

'It's a marriage of convenience,' she said, trying to stop the sudden panic running through her.

'But it's meant to look real. If we don't do anything fun on our honeymoon, surely it'll look suspicious?'

She didn't dare ask him what his idea of fun was. If it chimed with hers, she'd really be in trouble.

He smiled. 'Besides, just because it's fake, it doesn't mean we can't enjoy it.'

The pictures that put inside her head stopped any words at all coming out. And that scared her even more. Since Luke, she hadn't let herself think about dating, kissing or making love. She'd buried herself in work, because in her view work was a lot more reliable than relationships.

'You can show me all the things you love about Lark Hill,' he continued. 'Your favourite bits of Edinburgh.'

Sharing with him.

Being like a proper couple.

Part of Catriona yearned for it. The Dominic she was getting to know was the kind of man she'd like to be with. Quick mind, absurd humour, seriously attractive.

The way he was looking at her made her wonder if it was the same for him. If he was seeing past her professional face to who she really was, deep inside. And that was even more terrifying.

She stared at him mutely, not knowing what to say.

'Catriona. No strings,' he said gently.

This whole thing had been her idea in the first place.

So why did it suddenly feel as if she'd completely lost her judgement?

CHAPTER FOUR

WHAT HAD HE said to make her look so tense? Dominic wondered. Had it been suggesting taking her to a gig? Or was it the idea of having fun on their honeymoon that rattled her?

But he'd agreed to help her, and he wouldn't go back on his word.

'Ready for a bit more walking?' he asked. Moving helped him think better, and right now he felt as if he needed all the help he could get.

'Great idea. I'll sort the bill,' she said, and disappeared before he could suggest going halves.

If she was like this with him now, they'd never convince her half-brothers that their marriage was real.

How was he going to get her to relax with him?

When she reappeared, they headed back out to the river. She didn't initiate conversation, and the silence between them felt more and more awkward. In the end, he stopped dead. They might as well face the problem head-on. 'Catriona. This isn't going to work.'

She lifted her chin. 'You're right. And I'm sorry. I shouldn't have asked you to help me.'

'No, I mean if we're going to convince people that we're married for real, we need to…connect.' He grimaced. 'That isn't how I meant it to sound. I'm not being sleazy. I mean we need to be a bit more relaxed with each other.'

'To be honest, this isn't really in my skillset,' she said. 'And, learning what I have so far, it's unfair to you—and to your family. You're close to them. They'll be hurt if you don't invite them to your wedding.'

He liked the fact that, even though she wasn't close to her own family, she could appreciate how his family might feel about him getting married. 'They'll be fine about it if I tell them the truth,' he said. 'And your family's unlikely to be in touch with mine, so we won't have any issues with my family accidentally outing us. I'm assuming you don't have a big social media presence.'

She shook her head. 'Nothing that's outside the office. Social media's not really my sort of thing.'

He wasn't surprised. It wasn't really his, either. 'Then it's not going to be a problem.'

'This whole thing is a mess,' she said. 'But getting married is the only way to keep Lark Hill going.'

'If your dad had been still alive and he'd been the heir,' Dominic said, 'would anyone have been surprised if he'd sold up?'

'No,' she admitted. 'But I'm not my father. And I won't judge myself by his standards. It's not so much what other people think of me and what I do—it's what *I* think of me. I couldn't forgive myself if I let everyone down.'

She set high standards, he thought—and she reserved the highest ones for herself. Part of him wanted to give her a hug, and tell her to relax a bit, but he was pretty sure that would be the quickest way to make her barriers shoot straight back up again. He tried a different tack. 'Would you forgive anyone else, in your shoes?' he asked.

She spread her hands. 'That's academic, because it isn't anyone else. It's *my* responsibility.'

Time to back off. 'OK.' He gestured to the path ahead. 'Shall we?'

They walked on. The silence between them still wasn't companionable, but it wasn't completely awkward, either. It was more as if they were giving each other space to think and work out how they felt.

When they eventually stopped at another café just past Battersea Power Station on the other side of the river, Catriona asked, 'Are you completely sure you want to go ahead with this,

Dominic? Because the divorce will mean you can't get married in a church when you meet the love of your life.'

Something he'd never found and wasn't looking for. Or hadn't been, until now. The fact she'd asked unsettled him slightly. Did he want a grand, passionate love? Or was he content to be focused on his job, the way he'd been until now? 'I'm thirty-five,' he said. 'How likely is it that I'm going to meet someone?'

She frowned. 'At the risk of fuelling your ego, you're reasonably good-looking—don't women queue up to date you?'

So she found him physically attractive, too? That sent a very pleasurable flutter down his spine. 'Thanks for the compliment, but I'm happy as I am,' he said. 'I'm focusing on my career. In a way, you're doing me a favour because marrying you takes me off the market and saves me a few dull explanations.'

'We're on the same page, then,' she said. 'We need to make some plans. Prenups and booking the register office.'

Between them, they agreed which firms they were going to use for the prenups, and settled on the register office closest to their office: Camden Town Hall, just behind the station at King's Cross. Luckily, Catriona lived in the area for that particular office, so they didn't have to give notice in a different place. And trust her to have a handle on the smallest details, he thought.

'Which room do you want?' He angled his phone so she could see the page. The iconic marble staircase was listed as an option for just the bride, groom and two witnesses; or there was a small room with plush sofas and a neutral décor for a slightly larger group.

'I'd prefer the more private option,' she said. 'That staircase is beautiful, but it feels very… *public.*'

His thoughts exactly. 'We'll book the small room, then.' He paused. 'Are you absolutely sure you want to do it this way?

She nodded. 'There's no point in making a fuss when it's not a real wedding.'

He wondered if that bothered her—if she'd dreamed of a wedding when she was young, the way his sisters had. But he knew that asking her would just make her close up on him, and he wanted to break down the barriers between them, not add to them.

He scrolled down the list. 'There's a slot at three o'clock tomorrow. Does that work for you?'

She checked her diary. 'I have a phone call booked in with a client, but I can move it.'

'My afternoon of paperwork can fit round anything,' he said, and booked the appointment. Now what?

She was looking twitchy, as if she didn't know what to do now, either.

Weird how they seemed to unsettle each other. Though he was pretty sure she'd deny it if he raised the subject, and he didn't want her to know that she could fluster him. At the end of the day, she was still his rival at work. Showing weakness would be a bad tactical move. He'd think about it and find a better way to get her to open up. 'I guess we ought to do more of the dossier stuff,' he said instead.

'Maybe we can do it in chunks?' she asked. 'I don't think I can face doing any more of that today.'

'Maybe we can make a list of questions,' he said.

'Good idea. We'll swap lists tomorrow.'

'Sure.'

'I…um…guess I'll see you at work in the morning,' she said.

Right then, she looked really vulnerable, he thought. And, yes, maybe she was from a privileged class: but that didn't mean she was facing something easy now. Dealing with her grief at losing the last member of her family she'd been close to, having to give up the partnership she'd worked hard for, shouldering the responsibilities of her grandfather's estate, and having to handle what sounded like a difficult family.

Going to boarding school at the age of seven was probably what had made her so self-sufficient, but he still had the distinct impression that Catriona was lonely. Whereas he could pick up the phone and call a dozen people who'd be straight by his side if he asked, he had the feeling she didn't have anyone.

Poor little rich girl.

Though what he felt about her wasn't pity. She intrigued him; now he was starting to get to know her, he realised that she wasn't who he'd thought she was. The real Catriona, the one she kept hidden, was someone he thought he could actually like. More than like, if he was honest about it: the glitter in her eyes and the suspicion of a dimple when she smiled made a wave of heat wash through him.

'I'll walk you to the Tube,' he said.

'You really don't have to.'

'I know you're perfectly capable of looking after yourself.' He suspected she'd had to do that for a very, very long time. 'But it's the way I was brought up. Humour me,' he said. 'I'm guessing you've had enough socialising for today, so we don't have to make small talk. But I'll walk with you.'

Those ice-blue eyes softened slightly with what he thought might be gratitude. 'Thank you.'

He did exactly as he'd said, walking with her

to Pimlico tube station without making her talk about something deep or irritating her with small talk. Their trains home were on different lines, so he said goodbye to her on the station concourse and headed for his flat.

Later that evening, he rang his mum to let her know what was going on.

'Are you sure this is a good idea, love?' Ginny asked.

'Yes. It means I get the promotion.'

'But is that the way you really want to do it? I mean, getting *married*—that's a huge thing,' she said.

'I know. I didn't want you to get the wrong idea and think I've fallen in love,' he said.

'That's the only reason why you should get married—because you love each other,' Ginny said. 'Don't let what happened with your dad put you off marriage. Our Tilly's happy. And Suzy's hinted that she and Lou might be moving in together. I wouldn't be surprised if there was a wedding on the cards there, too.'

Dominic coughed. 'What about you and Ray?'

'We're fine as we are,' she said immediately.

'I rest my case, Mum,' he said.

'Love, I know we were lucky and people helped us when we needed it most,' Ginny said, 'but you've more than paid that back with all the *pro bono* work you do. You don't have to get married.'

'It's a business deal, Mum, I make partner if I do this. It means financial security for all of us.' Though, at the same time, he knew there was a little more to it than that. Now Catriona had started to let him see a glimpse of who she was beneath the painted hoardings, he discovered that he was intrigued by her.

'When's the date of the wedding?' Ginny asked.

'About a month. I'll let you know the exact date once we've been to the register office tomorrow,' he said.

'Who are going to be your witnesses?' she asked.

'We'll ask two strangers off the street,' he said.

'Absolutely not,' Ginny said. 'If you're going through with this, then I want to be there—and so will Ray. And Tilly and Suzy. And Joe and Lou. And baby Aiden.'

'But—'

'No buts,' she said firmly. 'Catriona needs to be there for the family video call on Wednesday. We want to meet her.'

'Mum, the whole point of me telling you about it now is because it's not a real wedding. It's so she can sort out her family business and I get the partnership,' Dominic said. 'You don't need to meet her and you don't need to drag all the way over to London to be our witness.'

'It's not negotiable,' Ginny said. 'I'll speak to you on Wednesday. And your sisters,' she warned, 'might want to talk to you before that.'

They did. Tilly and Suzy tag-teamed him in a video call, and both of them raised the same arguments as their mum had.

In the end, he said, 'I've always supported you both in what you want to do. Can't you do the same for me?'

'But you're not doing this for *you*, Dommy, are you?' Suzy protested.

'We're helping each other. The deal is she gets the castle, and she steps out of the partnership race to leave the way clear for me.'

'You would probably have won that anyway,' Tilly pointed out.

'Thanks for the vote of confidence, Tillykins, but there are no guarantees I would've got it,' Dominic said. 'If I had to choose between us, I'd find it a tough call. And do you know what this means? A uni fund for Aiden, at the very least. And I can pay off Mum's mortgage. Build that extension for you. Give our Suze a hand with the deposit on a flat.' Tilly, who'd clearly been trying to interrupt him, closed her mouth. He'd finally found the way to show her that the partnership would do a lot for all of them.

'I still think it's a bad idea,' Suzy said, 'but we'll be fair and hear what she has to say on Wednesday.'

Dominic knew he was going to have to explain a few things to Catriona before she spoke to his sisters. 'All right. I'll talk to you then,' he said.

On Monday, Catriona and Dominic left the office at different times, headed in different directions, and met at the register office five minutes before their appointment.

'We need to talk before we do this,' Dominic said.

Catriona felt her stomach twist. 'You've changed your mind?'

'No, but I told my mum last night.'

She schooled her expression to what she hoped was careful neutrality. 'And?'

'She doesn't think it's a great idea, but she'll support us.' He wrinkled his nose. 'You know we said we'd pick witnesses off the street?'

'Yes.'

'It seems that's superfluous to requirements.'

She narrowed her eyes at him. 'How?'

'We have six and a half witnesses,' he said.

'Six and a *half*?' She didn't quite understand.

'My mother and her partner, my sisters and their partners—and my nephew. Aiden isn't old enough to understand or even speak yet, but he'll be with Tilly and Joe. He's the half.'

Her quiet, businesslike wedding was rapidly turning into something else, and her chest felt tight.

'I'm afraid I haven't quite finished. You know I have a weekly video call with my mum and my sisters? They want you to be there for it, this week.'

Catriona frowned. 'Why? Don't they know it's a business arrangement?'

'That doesn't change anything.' He flicked into the message app on his phone and handed it to her. 'See for yourself.'

The messages from his sisters made it very clear they expected to meet her.

She winced. 'I'm sorry for causing a row with your family.'

'There's no row,' he said. 'But I was thinking: my sisters are both on social media. They know I want to be partner, so they'll help us if it means I get what I want. They'll post the sort of things that will convince your family that this is real.' The horror she felt must've shown on her expression, because he said, 'You don't have to go on social media yourself. Though it'd probably be useful for Lark Hill to have social media accounts, once we've decided on the way forward.'

We again.

But they weren't really a 'we', were they? She was on her own, the way she'd always been. 'Maybe,' she said.

'They've already pointed out that we need an engagement ring.'

She shrugged. 'We can use my grandmother's engagement ring.'

'You don't want something just for you?'

She thought of Luke. How he'd swept her off her feet and bought her an expensive flashy diamond, even though secretly she would've preferred a smaller and prettier ring, like her grandmother's. She'd given the flashy diamond back to him, along with all the things he'd left at her flat. 'No,' she said. 'I like my grandmother's ring, actually.'

'At least let me buy the wedding rings.'

'Provided they're plain, and not expensive.'

He looked at her. 'You don't wear much jewellery, do you?'

'Just a watch and earrings.' She gestured to the pearl studs in her ears. 'My grandparents gave me these on my twenty-first.'

He raised an eyebrow. 'Is that something to do with your mother?'

He was sharp to have picked that up, Catriona thought. 'Let's just say "dripping with diamonds" would describe her perfectly,' she said dryly. 'That's not me.'

'OK. We'll do it your way,' he said.

Thankfully, there was a space in the schedule for one of the small rooms on the date they wanted, so they were able to book the room for Tuesday the fifth of December as well as sort out the paperwork.

'What's the situation with your prenups?' she asked as they left the register office.

'I briefed them first thing this morning. They should be back at the end of tomorrow afternoon,' he said.

'Good. Same with mine,' she said.

'Business meeting after work tomorrow?'

She nodded. 'Plus. I need to see Lewis—' the managing partner of their firm '—this afternoon to sort out my sabbatical.' She held his gaze. 'And to withdraw from the partnership opportunity.'

Fulfilling the terms of their deal. She was giving up so much for the castle. Dominic hoped it was worth it, for her sake. 'Thank you. I assume we're going back to the office separately.'

'Yes. It's pointless fuelling the office grapevine. I'll message you later.' Her face looked slightly pinched, 'And thank you, Dominic. You've helped this all be less—well, painful.'

And all of a sudden his heart ached for her. 'Did you want to invite your family to the wedding?'

'There's no point,' she said. 'My mother will be busy.'

Too busy to attend her daughter's wedding? How selfish could the woman get? Well, he already knew that Catriona's mother had left her daughter's upbringing to boarding school and her in-laws. Dominic couldn't understand it; his own mother would drop everything if one of her children needed her. Catriona's mother needed a reality check, he thought grimly. Or maybe Catriona really was better off without her.

She messaged him later that afternoon to suggest meeting at seven the following evening—to give them both a chance to read through each other's prenups. He'd just bet she'd stay late in the office.

He messaged back.

Fine by me. How did it go with the partners?

They're giving me the year's sabbatical I asked for. And I kept my side of the bargain; I'm surprised they haven't already asked you in to discuss the partnership.

Almost the second after he'd read Catriona's message, the managing partner's PA rang him to ask him to see Lewis in his office.

This was it.

The moment he'd worked so hard for.

He'd finally reached the pinnacle.

And he was shocked to find his stomach full of butterflies.

The managing partner smiled when Dominic walked in. 'Congratulations are in order, Dominic. I'll cut to the chase. We've been very pleased with your work and we're delighted to offer you a partnership.'

It was everything Dominic wanted. A partnership in a prestigious firm of London solicitors. He'd be able to support his family, just the way he'd always planned.

Of course he was going to accept the partnership.

Though he'd expected to feel differently when he'd achieved his goal. As if he were walking on air, triumphant, instead of this weird flatness seeping through him.

He had a pretty good idea what was at the root of his feelings. *Second-best.* The words echoed in his head. And he needed to know. 'If Catriona hadn't ruled herself out of the running, would you still be talking to me?' he asked.

'That's very direct,' Lewis said.

Dominic simply waited.

'You obviously know Catriona's stepped down,' Lewis said.

'I also know why,' Dominic said. 'And that she's taking a year's sabbatical.'

'Interesting,' Lewis said. 'We were all rather under the impression that you and Catriona were deadly rivals.'

They had been. But everything had changed over the last few days. 'You haven't answered my question.'

'It's a moot point.' Lewis smiled at the legal pun.

'Not to me.'

'We hadn't quite decided,' Lewis said. 'It was very, very close.'

'In other words, no.'

Lewis sighed. 'It was very, very close,' he said again. 'We really hadn't decided. It could've gone either way.'

'Then maybe,' Dominic said, 'we need to have a slightly different conversation.'

Lewis blinked. 'You're turning down the partnership?'

The hint of dismay in the managing partner's eyes, quickly masked, made Dominic feel a bit better. Maybe he wasn't second-best, after all. 'No.' That was the point of his deal with Catriona: that he'd get the partnership. 'But it's unfair that Catriona's personal circumstances should disadvantage her, when the situation's not of her making.'

'What exactly are you suggesting?' Lewis asked.

'In a year's time, you'd potentially have space for two partners: ones who bring very different but equal abilities to the table. I'm better at overview and strategy, but she's better at details.'

Lewis raised an eyebrow. 'Your point?'

If Lewis valued him enough to make him partner, then so would quite a lot of other people in London. Which put Dominic in precisely the negotiation position he needed. 'If the decision was so close, why choose between us at all? Particularly when our skills complement each other. Make me a partner now, and promote Catriona when she's back from her sabbatical.'

'I see,' Lewis said. 'That's very gallant of you.'

'It's a business decision,' Dominic said. 'She'd be an excellent partner.'

'Do you think she would've suggested the same, if your positions had been reversed?' Lewis asked.

Dominic thought of the way Catriona had told him how she wanted to get the estate to work—without ripping off her tenants or cutting out her half-brothers. 'Yes, actually. I do.'

Lewis was silent for a moment, and then sighed. 'I agree. She would. And you have a point. It's what's made it so difficult to choose between you.'

'I'm glad you see things the way I do,' Dominic said.

Lewis rested his elbows on his desk and steepled his fingers. 'All right. I'll need to talk to the rest of the partners.'

'But they'll be guided by your view. Which is that two partners with a broad skillset between them will make an unbeatable team.' Dominic smiled.

'And that,' Lewis said, 'is exactly why you'll make an excellent partner. You see the bigger picture. Welcome to the team.' Lewis smiled. 'And I'll talk to the partners and then Catriona, in due course.'

'Thank you,' Dominic said. 'And perhaps we can hold off announcing my news until she's on sabbatical. Otherwise it feels like gloating.'

'Quite the moral compass you have there,' Lewis said dryly.

'Added strength,' Dominic said, smiling. 'You don't build a strong team by trampling on them. You do it by empowering them.'

CHAPTER FIVE

THE FOLLOWING EVENING, Dominic met Catriona at a wine bar far enough from the office that they were unlikely to bump into a colleague. He bought them both a glass of white wine, and they found a quiet spot.

'Have you had a chance to look through everything?' he asked.

'Yes. Have you?'

He nodded. 'I'm happy.'

'Ditto. Though I notice you've asked for a clause to make it clear that you're not responsible for Lark Hill or the mortgage on my flat, and I'm not responsible for the mortgage on your flat,' she said.

'So our assets will be separated.'

'It's the wording you've used,' she said. 'What haven't you told me?'

He should've known she'd pick that up. Her eye for detail. 'I guess I should disclose this—and you need to know the whole story before tomorrow,' he said, 'but this is about my family and I want to keep it confidential.'

'I'd never gossip about you.'

He knew that, but he remembered what it was like to be talked about. The way the other mums at school had avoided his mum at the school gate. The whispers. The shame. It still made him feel slightly sick.

'My father left us when Mum was pregnant with Suzy.' He looked away. 'He had a gambling problem. I know addiction is an illness, and I should feel sorry for him, but I just can't. Not after what he did to Mum.' He looked her straight in the eye. 'He hadn't paid the mortgage for months, and he'd hidden all the mortgage company's letters so she didn't have a clue that they were in so much debt or were near to the house being repossessed. He'd also wiped out their joint savings and maxed out their joint overdraft.'

Catriona winced. 'All their finances were in joint names?'

'Yes. When he walked out on Mum and left the country with another woman—someone he'd met in the casino—he also left her with all the debt.' He closed his eyes for a moment. 'Our house was repossessed the week after Mum gave birth to Suzy.'

'That,' she said, 'was incredibly unfair. And surely there's something in the rules that says you can't make a new mother homeless?'

'You'd think,' he said. 'Though, even without

all the extra debt from the missed payments, Mum couldn't afford the mortgage on her own. Despite the fact that she wasn't the one who'd run up the debts, she was liable for them because they were in joint names. My father had skipped the country, so she was the easiest one for the bank to go after.' He frowned. 'The local solicitor gave her some advice, *pro bono*. She had the joint account frozen. But, even when the house was sold, the money wasn't enough to pay off the debts. She ended up having to declare bankruptcy. My grandparents and my aunts and uncles did what they could to help with babysitting, and my grandparents made sure we always had food on the table, but Mum hated the fact she had to rely on them for help.'

'None of it was her fault.' She looked at him. 'Your mum sounds an amazing woman.'

'She is.' He was fiercely proud of her.

'That's why you really do the *pro bono* work in family law, isn't it?' she asked. 'Not just to balance out the corporate stuff, like you told me, but because someone helped your family when you needed it most, and you're paying it forward.'

Again, Catriona had zeroed in on the salient point. 'Yes. Though if you tell anyone that I'll deny it.'

'I wouldn't drag your family into it,' she said. 'I'm sorry they had a tough time—and I'm not surprised you're fed up with me whining about inheriting a castle.'

'You're not whining. You're trying to do the right thing.' He raised an eyebrow. 'Before you asked me to marry you, I thought you were rich, spoiled and entitled.'

She nodded her head slowly. 'That's fair,' she said. 'It's probably what I am.'

He shook his head. 'You come from a rich family—but nobody spoiled you. And you're not entitled.'

'Before I asked you to marry me,' she said, 'I thought you were ambitious and probably in the job just for the money. But the money isn't for you, is it? It's about being able to support your family.'

'And never being in a position again where I have to rely on the kindness of other people,' he said. 'And you want to help your half-brothers. Except it sounds to me as if they're the ones who are spoiled and entitled.'

'They seem to be, at the moment, but I'm hoping it's partly because they haven't worked out who they really are yet. My father seemed to go for a particular type of woman, so they're going to have to work pretty hard to battle the selfish genes.' She gave him a wry smile. 'They weren't sent to stay at Lark Hill, the way I was, so they never really got to know our grandparents and they don't see the castle the way I do.'

'If I were in your shoes, I'd get married to inherit the castle,' he said.

'If I were in your shoes…' She paused. 'I hope I'd be decent enough to help you.'

'You would be,' he said, meaning it. He'd learned that she had a strong moral compass, and he liked that. Liked *her*. 'Funny. Last week we probably wouldn't have chosen to work together. This week, we're planning our wedding.'

She chuckled and it was a sound he was quickly becoming to appreciate. He'd love to hear it more and see her loosening up when she was with him.

'Acting as a team. Weird, indeed,' she said. 'Thank you for being honest with me, Dominic. I can see why you don't have any time for your father.' She paused. 'Did he ever apologise, or try to pay any of the money back to your mum?'

'No.'

'That's atrocious. If he ever comes back into this country, I want to know and I'll make sure he sees justice in court,' she said. 'And I'll personally see to it that he apologises. Sincerely.'

Dominic was pleased that she was immediately on his mother's side. 'Being married to me means there would be a conflict of interest and you couldn't be on the prosecution's team,' he reminded her.

'Then we'll brief someone we trust to do it for us,' she said.

We.

Was she, too, starting to see them as a team?

'Sounds good to me,' he said. 'I was thinking, tomorrow night you might as well come and have dinner at my flat before the call. Is there anything you don't eat?'

'No allergies and I'm not fussy,' she said. 'Can I bring wine or pudding?'

'I'm not much of a pudding person,' he said. 'You don't need to bring anything. Just yourself.'

'All right,' she said. 'What time?'

'Seven? It'll give us time to eat and plan our strategy before the call,' he said. Though it wasn't just that, was it? If he was honest with himself, it meant he'd be able to spend a bit more time just with her.

'Works for me,' she said.

There was a pinker tinge than normal to her cheeks. Was she, too, starting to want to spend time with him? Or was he just fooling himself, confused by an attraction he'd never expected to feel?

She glanced at her watch. 'I'll see you tomorrow, then. Let me know your address. And we'll get everything signed by Friday.'

* * *

On Wednesday evening, Catriona felt oddly nervous. She really should've checked the dress code with Dominic. Her office suit clearly wouldn't pass muster with his family, but jeans felt too casual. In the end, she went for a simple black woollen dress.

Dominic's flat was part of a converted yellow-brick warehouse overlooking the river. When she pressed the door intercom, he buzzed her through. 'I'm on the third floor,' he said. 'There's a lift or stairs—your choice.'

She took the lift; he greeted her at his front door—wearing jeans and a round-necked cream sweater, which made her feel overdressed. But what did you wear when you 'met' your convenient husband-to-be's family for the first time on a video call?

'Welcome,' he said.

'Thank you.' She took a box of good crackers, a bunch of black grapes and a paper-wrapped package from her bag. 'My contribution to dinner,' she said.

He raised an eyebrow. 'I did say you needn't bring anything.'

'Remember when you insisted on walking me to the tube station on Sunday when I said you didn't need to, and you asked me to humour you because it was the way you were brought up?'

she asked. 'This is the same thing. My grandparents always taught me to take a gift for my host or hostess. You're not into sweet things, so I couldn't bring chocolates, and flowers didn't feel right. Humour me.'

'All right. Thank you.' He sniffed the package. 'Ooh. Would I be right in thinking this contains a very nice ripe Camembert?'

'At perfect ooziness,' she said.

'Wonderful. Thank you very much indeed. I can always be won round by cheese.' He grinned. 'There's another product idea for you: Lark Hill cheese.'

She didn't think that grin was for show: this was the real Dominic, the man behind the professional at work, full of enthusiasm.

And he was still thinking of things to help the castle, even without her asking. It made her feel as if he was becoming as invested in the project as she was—and not just because it meant he'd make partner. He was doing it because they were a team.

Which was scary and thrilling, all at the same time.

'Let me put this in the kitchen. Feel free to hang your coat up. Then I'll give you the tour.'

She hung her coat on the rack by his front door and followed him into the galley-style kitchen. The flooring was stripped oak planks, the cupboards were shiny white, the walls were painted a soft duck-egg-blue and the worktops were mid-grey granite. Everywhere was incredibly tidy; only the kettle was on display on the worktops.

'The bathroom's opposite,' he said, gesturing to the doorway. 'The living room's through here.' The room was an enormous square; one wall was almost entirely glass, with French doors and blinds she guessed were for sunny days. There were two comfortable-looking sofas; against one wall was a desk, next to a bookcase, which she could see was stuffed with a mixture of legal text-books and the crime novels he'd told her were his favourites. There was a cabinet next to the book-case, stuffed full of vinyl albums, with a turntable on top; an electro-acoustic guitar and amp sat on the other side. Six chairs were tucked neatly around a dining table, which was set for two.

On the neutral-painted walls, there were a couple of seascapes, which looked to her like original watercolours rather than prints; on the mantelpiece, there was a scattering of framed photographs, all showing Dominic with his fam-ily—everything from his formal graduation pic-ture to candid snaps in the garden. They were the kind of pictures she didn't have, apart from her graduation photograph with her grandparents, and she pushed down the wave of longing. His family wasn't going to become her family, she reminded herself. Not when their wedding was just for convenience. She was perfectly fine on her own. Always had been.

'It's a very nice flat,' she said.

'I like it,' he said. 'There's a communal garden—not that I really get time to use it—and the balcony is lovely in summer.' He gestured to the French doors. 'The view's pretty good.'

The river was ink-dark at this time of night, with lights reflected in the water. Catriona recognised the lit-up shapes of the Shard and the Fenchurch Building. 'I bet this is stunning at sunrise and sunset.'

'It is,' he said. 'I tend to keep the blinds open, except when it's blazingly hot.'

'Mine's a duplex on the top two floors, so I don't have a garden either,' she said. 'Just a terrace with a few pots of geraniums and the like. Though it's only a few steps to Regent's Park, so I can wander through the rose gardens and up Primrose Hill whenever I want.'

'That sounds good, too,' he said.

'I noticed your record collection, by the way. Would that be your Uncle Bill's influence?'

'And the guitar, yes.' He smiled. 'He taught me years ago that vinyl sounds so much better than digital.'

'With all the scratches and hisses?'

'You don't lose bits of information, the way

you do with an MP3 that has to translate analogue to digital and back again,' he said. 'And the sound's warmer. Can I get you a glass of wine?'

'If you have camomile tea,' she said, 'that would be perfect.'

He grimaced. 'Afraid not. I can do builder's tea.'

She shook her head. 'Then a glass of water would be lovely, thanks.'

'Have a seat,' he said, gesturing to the table.

Dinner turned out to be a seriously good chicken tagine scattered with pomegranate seeds and pieces of preserved lemon, served with greens and some fluffy couscous. 'This is really lovely,' she said, impressed by his cooking skills.

'Thanks. I like messing about in the kitchen. It relaxes me,' he said.

She raised an eyebrow. 'Your kitchen's spotless. There's not even the tiniest hint of mess.'

'If you'd seen it half an hour ago, you wouldn't be saying that,' he said with a grin.

Oh, that grin. It was boyish, slightly goofy, and it made her heart feel as if it had done a somersault.

Which was ridiculous. And she wasn't supposed to be thinking about him in those terms. Their marriage had nothing to do with any foolish feelings of attraction, and everything to do with sorting out her grandfather's estate.

'Are you OK?' he asked.

'I'm a bit nervous about meeting your family,' she admitted.

'They'll be fine. Well, they might grill you a bit,' he said. 'But that's because they're worried about me.' He rolled his eyes. 'Despite the fact I've explained the situation to them.'

Which didn't reassure her in the slightest. What if one of them decided to object formally at the wedding?

'Maybe we should've eloped to Las Vegas,' she said.

'They would've given you a harder time if we'd got married without telling them,' he countered.

All the same, her stomach was tied in knots by the time the video call took place. And it seemed that his sisters had congregated at their mother's house because only one screen came up on his laptop.

'Catriona, this is my mum Ginny, my baby sister Suzy, and my middle sister Tilly with my nephew Aiden,' Dominic said, introducing them swiftly. 'Everyone, this is Catriona.'

'Hello,' Catriona said.

'Nice to meet you,' Ginny said, though her tone was slightly reserved.

Suzy was the one to raise the tough issue. 'Dommy says you have to get married or you can't inherit the castle and it'll go to your half-brothers instead.'

Which sounded horrible.

'It's not about greed,' Catriona said. 'It means the tenants won't have to worry about a change in ownership that might lead to a rent increase or even giving them notice, and the castle stays in my family instead of being sold off to the highest bidder.'

'But you're both supposed to be hotshot lawyers,' Tilly said. 'You were Dominic's main competition for the partnership.'

Catriona flushed. 'Yes.'

'Then why can't you find a loophole to get round the will?' Tilly asked.

'Because there *isn't* a loophole,' Dominic said.

'And he said you don't get on very well, because you're rich and ent—'

'Tills, drop it,' Dominic cut in, looking pained.

'She's right. We need to be open about this. Yes, in the past Dominic and I rubbed each other up the wrong way professionally,' Catriona said. 'We're both focused on work and we both think we're always right. Obviously we've clashed.'

'And you chose him as the one to marry?' Suzy asked.

'He has integrity,' Catriona said; glancing at the man who very soon would become her husband. 'I trust him.' She wasn't lying; she did trust him and that was something she hadn't done for a long time. Not since she'd discovered Luke's betrayal…

'And you're giving up the partnership race for him?' Tilly asked.

'This way we both get what we want,' Catriona said.

Ginny looked thoughtful. 'Will this be the first time your family's ever heard of Dommy?'

'Yes,' Catriona admitted.

'In their shoes,' Ginny said, 'I'd suspect this was a fake marriage so you can meet the terms of the will, and I'd contest it.'

'The castle needs extensive repairs. We can't afford a court case,' Catriona added, 'which is why I need to convince them it's a real marriage.'

'Are they coming to the wedding?' Tilly asked.

Catriona winced. 'No. Just the three of you, your partners and the baby.'

'What about your mum?' Tilly asked.

At Catriona's headshake, Suzy frowned. 'There's nobody on your side?'

'My best friend moved to New York six months ago. And she's pregnant, so I don't want to drag her over here on a plane. This is going to be a quiet wedding,' Catriona said. 'Which I think most people would understand, given that I buried my grandfather a couple of weeks ago.'

'My condolences,' Ginny said, and it seemed genuine.

'I trust her, too. I told her about our situation with my father,' Dominic said.

'And I'll respect that confidence. I'm sorry you had a rough time,' Catriona said.

'It is what it is. Gambling's an addiction, and addiction's an illness,' Ginny said. 'The man I married would never have neglected his children or cheated on me. The gambling changed him.'

'I would still have wanted to punch him on the nose for what he did,' Catriona said.

Ginny gave her a wry smile. 'I wanted to, believe me. But my focus was on the kids. And I was lucky that my family helped us.'

What would it be like to have a family that pulled together like that? Catriona wondered. Not that she'd ever know.

'You're going to need help convincing your brothers,' Tilly said. 'What are you wearing?'

'My work clothes will be fine,' Catriona said.

'That wouldn't convince me,' Suzy said. 'You need to wear something that looks a *bit* bridal. Skip the veil, but you need flowers.'

'Agreed,' Tilly said. 'What are you doing on Sunday?'

'I…' Catriona couldn't think of an excuse quickly enough.

'Good. You're coming to Birmingham,' Tilly said. 'We'll go shopping.'

'But—'

'You don't have time?' Suzy asked. 'Then we'll order some things in your size. Lou can do a trial run of your hair and make-up, and her best friend's a florist so she can sort out the flowers. And then, on the day, you throw your bouquet at Lou.' She gave Catriona a broad wink. 'Which is a discussion for another time.'

'Bring a couple of pairs of shoes with different heel heights with you,' Tilly added with a smile, 'so then you'll know what shoes to get to go with the dress.'

'I know it's not our planned weekend for Sunday lunch, but I'll cook,' Ginny said.

'Talking of food, what about the wedding breakfast?' Suzy asked.

'We hadn't planned one. It was meant to be a quiet wedding with just the two of us and two witnesses off the street,' Dominic said. 'Stop steamrollering my fiancée.'

His fiancée.

And he was standing up for her.

Catriona was perfectly capable of standing up for herself—and she knew that Dominic knew it, too—but she kind of liked the way he'd taken her part. And she liked his family. Yes, they were a bit over the top, and their reaction to the whole situation was ridiculous enough to make her smile; but they were enthusiastic, and they clearly loved Dominic to bits. This was the kind of family she could enjoy being part of—except this wasn't a real relationship.

'It's not about steamrollering,' Tilly said. 'You're getting married in four weeks. In December. Most places will be booked up with Christmas lunches. But you absolutely can't get married without at least having lunch. What time's the wedding?'

'One o'clock,' Dominic said.

'Maybe just book somewhere nice for lunch at two, so we can toast you with bubbles—and then you'll have the photos to show your brothers, Trina,' Suzy said.

Trina?

Nobody had ever shortened her name.

But Catriona didn't have time even to think about how that made her feel, because then Tilly asked, 'Are you officially engaged yet?'

'That's going to be on Friday,' Dominic said.

'You've chosen the ring?' Suzy asked.

'We're using my grandmother's,' Catriona said.

'That's nice. Tradition. And you'll be sure to post it on social media,' Tilly said. 'Maybe with a picture of your grandparents at their engagement, if you've got one.'

'I don't do social media,' Catriona said. The idea of it made her skin itch. Why did you need to have your life on display for other people? Why put yourself up to be judged?

'You need to convince your brothers,' Suzy said. 'Play it safe and take pictures on your phone.'

How daunting it all felt.

Dominic clearly realised that Catriona had had enough, because he said, 'OK, guys. Grilling over. We'll see you on Sunday.'

Catriona had just about enough presence of mind to say goodbye, but her mind was reeling when Dominic ended the call.

'Sorry. I'm used to the way they are, but it looks as if you found them a bit much,' he said.

A bit much? His family was *terrifying*. But they were also caring and kind. Enchanting. Not that she wanted to tell him. She wasn't ready to expose all her weaknesses. 'I can see where you get your energy from,' she said instead. She raised an eyebrow. 'And the bossiness.'

He grinned. 'Why, thank you, Fifi.' But then his smile faded and he took her hand and squeezed it briefly.

Her skin felt as if it shimmered where he'd touched it, and little flickers of something she didn't want to name started low in her belly.

'I'll drive us on Sunday,' he said. 'I normally get the train home so I can do some work on the way, but if I drive it means we can escape whenever you need to, instead of being tied to the train timetable.'

She hadn't expected him to be so thoughtful—

or to realise that, coming from a family that was as distant as you could get, it was likely that she'd find a family like his overwhelming. 'Thank you. I'll—um—see you tomorrow.'

'Have you got a taxi booked?'

'Tube,' she said. Before he could offer to walk her to the tube station, she added, 'And the walk on my own will help me get my head round things. Thank you for dinner.' And then she left before she could land herself in an even deeper muddle.

By the time she got back to her flat, Catriona found Suzy and Tilly had already set her up in a WhatsApp group with them, and there was a screenful of messages. They were clearly taken with the idea of wedding planning—but beneath it was a kindness she found humbling. She was a stranger, and they were helping her. For their brother's sake, admittedly; but it was good to feel that she had a team.

She answered their questions, sent them a snap of the ring, and then sent a private message to Dominic.

Your sisters are lovely.

They have their moments. Tell me if they get too much.

All of this was too much. She'd sworn she'd never have a wedding again. But they were right: all of this was necessary to save Lark Hill. Her home. She'd just never expected to bring a whole new family into it. And then she smiled in spite of herself. Because clearly Dominic was a package deal, and that package was loud and brash… and unexpectedly wonderful.

CHAPTER SIX

On Thursday, Suzy and Tilly sent Catriona an array of dress pictures.

Suzy warned:

Don't show Dommy. It's bad luck for the groom to see the dress.

Even though it wasn't a proper wedding?

Catriona chose the plainest dresses, and sent her thanks.

On Friday lunchtime, she signed the prenups with Dominic, with their lawyers as witnesses; and on Friday evening they met up after work, ready to take an engagement photograph for her brothers—and, more importantly, their mothers. She'd assumed that they'd go to a bar somewhere—maybe one with a pretty flower wall, or fairy lights—or to dinner, but instead Dominic shepherded her to the Regent's Canal at Little Venice, where a boat was waiting for them.

'A private cruise?' she asked, surprised.

'It's been quite a week,' he said. 'I thought you might like the chance to chill out. Privately.'

'Thank you.' It was exactly what she needed. 'Has Lewis talked to you about the partnership yet?'

'Yes. When you're on leave, we'll announce the deal.' He looked her. 'Otherwise it feels like rubbing your nose in it.'

'That's decent of you,' she said.

He shrugged it off. 'You would have done the same.'

'Even though I'm an ambitious ball-breaker?'

'Now I know you better, I realise that isn't who you are,' he said. 'But you don't suffer fools gladly.'

'Not anymore.'

He raised an eyebrow. 'That sounds like an interesting story.'

'Dull,' she corrected. 'Maybe some other time.' She could see in his expression that he'd ask her about it at some time in the future. She'd make sure she was ready, with all the emotions taken out. Cold, hard facts. And proof that she learned from her mistakes.

He helped her onto the boat and introduced her to the captain. The covered viewing deck at the front of the boat was twined with twinkly fairy lights, and there was a huge fluffy blanket on the seat behind the table—clearly aimed at couples who wanted to snuggle up together. Which *wasn't* her and Dominic.

'It's so we don't freeze,' he said, seeing where she was looking. 'Given it's a November evening.'

'Uh-huh,' she said, sitting down and draping the blanket over her lap.

He sat down next to her, did the same, and then leaned to the side and brought out a willow hamper.

'I wasn't planning to starve you,' he said, and swiftly decanted the hamper's contents onto the table: a charcuterie and cheeseboard with crackers, mini plum tomatoes, olives and baby figs.

If this had been a real date, Catriona would definitely have been swept off her feet. As it was, she was just very close to it. This was one of the most romantic things anyone had ever done for her, and it was just the kind of food she enjoyed most.

'It's the perfect setting for an engagement,' she said. 'You've done a great job.'

'Thanks, though I haven't *quite* finished.' He flicked into a streaming app on his phone, and a few moments later gentle piano music floated into the air—the sort of music she really loved. He'd clearly remembered what she'd said.

Then he reached under the table and brought out two champagne flutes and a chilled bottle of champagne, deftly dealt with the cork and poured two glasses. He handed one to her, then raised his own glass in a toast. 'To you,' he said. 'Because you've changed the way I think about things, this last week.'

'You've changed the way I think, too,' she said. Particularly about him. How had she got him so wrong?

'I vote we eat before we do the taking-pictures-with-ring business,' he said.

'And I need to give you the ring anyway,' she said. She took the old-fashioned blue velvet box out of her bag and gave it to him.

'May I?' he asked.

'Sure.'

He opened the box. 'That's really pretty. Do you know how old it is?'

'It was my gran's, but she and Gramps married in the early sixties and I think this is Edwardian. It might have been her grandmother's,' Catriona said.

'What would she think of this wedding?'

'My grandmother was practical above all else,' she said. 'I think her marriage to Gramps was—well, dynastic, rather than a love match. But I'm pretty sure they grew to love each other. He missed her badly after she died.' And she missed both of them.

'To your grandparents,' he said, lifting his glass again.

'Grannie and Gramps,' she said, blinking back the threatening tears.

Once they'd finished the picnic—and most of the champagne—Dominic turned to her. 'Ready for this?'

'Ready,' she said.

He took the ring from the box and slid it onto her finger.

And this felt very, very different from the last time a man had slid an engagement ring onto her finger. This time, she wasn't in a spin and head over heels in love; but, this time, even though the engagement was fake, it felt real. As if Dominic was quietly making a promise that he intended to keep.

He took a photograph of the ring on her finger, and one of her holding her hand up in the traditional 'I said yes' pose.

'I've had instructions from the girls,' he said, pulling up a message on his phone. 'We need a shot of me holding your hand, ring uppermost.'

'OK,' she said.

He slid his palm underneath hers, and her skin tingled where he touched her. Which was crazy, because she and Dominic weren't in the least bit attracted to each other. She was just letting the situation sway her, she told herself. All the same, she found her fingers curling round his. And when she looked at him—were those little flecks of gold in his irises, or was it just a reflection of the fairy lights?

'And there's another one we have to do,' he said, carefully following the instructions in the text. 'Your left hand on my cheek to show off the ring. Me leaning in for a kiss. Both of us having our eyes closed.'

The tingling in her skin spread.

'Close your eyes,' he said. 'This is our first kiss as an engaged couple.'

Except they weren't a couple. They weren't really engaged. And was he *really* going to kiss her?

'Relax,' he said. 'Pretend I'm your dream man. The actor you fell in love with when you were fifteen.'

'I...' Her breath hitched.

'Relax,' he repeated. 'Just think about kissing someone you'd really, really want to kiss.'

The world felt as if it was tilting sideways when she realised that the person she was thinking of, right at that moment, was Dominic Ferrars.

'Imagine he's close,' Dominic whispered. 'Close enough for you to feel the heat of his skin next to yours. And any second now his mouth's going to touch yours. It's just the two of you. Under the stars on a deserted beach, with the water swishing softly across the sand.'

Catriona could hear water swishing and, even

though she knew it was the Regent's Canal rather than the sea, she could imagine that she was standing on a beach with her fiancé.

With Dominic.

'Think of that first touch of his mouth against yours. Soft, sweet, a declaration of love to seal your engagement,' he continued, his voice hypnotic.

With her eyes still closed, Catriona felt her lips parting and her head tipping back, inviting a kiss.

Dominic had no idea who Catriona was thinking of. But the softness in her face, the way she arched towards him with her eyes closed, was his undoing. He couldn't stop himself leaning towards her.

This was supposed to be for social media. For them to make an official declaration of their engagement to the world.

And instead it felt like an intensely private moment. As if the scenario he'd just suggested was true: the two of them, on a deserted beach, about to kiss. His mouth was millimetres from hers.

Dominic had just about enough presence of mind left to glance at the screen of his phone and check that they were somewhere in the right place for the photograph.

And then he closed his eyes and touched his mouth against hers.

It felt like an electric shock.

Particularly when she kissed him back, all sweet and enticing. Her mouth was so soft against his, and he wanted more. He wanted her to feel the same kind of sparks that were igniting in his head. He dropped his phone on the seat and drew her closer. The hand she'd rested on his cheek slid round to the back of his neck, and she opened her mouth, letting him deepen the kiss.

He'd kissed women before. Kissed women he liked. Kissed women he might've been able to love.

But kissing Catriona was like nothing else he'd ever experienced.

It felt so right.

And it shook him to the core.

When he finally broke the kiss, he stared at her. 'Um… Sorry. That wasn't supposed to happen.'

'Nothing happened,' she said swiftly. 'It was just for the photographs.'

But something *had* happened. There had been a connection between them he hadn't expected, and he was pretty sure it was the same for her, too. Her eyes were wide and her mouth was parted, her lips plump and tempting.

It flustered him; now he knew what it felt to kiss her, he wanted to do it again. And again. Until they were both dizzy.

Though was that longing or worry he saw in her eyes?

He couldn't be sure, so he backed off. 'Just for the photographs,' he echoed, knowing that he was lying and it had been a lot more than that.

Somehow he managed to make polite conversation through the rest of their boat trip. Once they were on land again, he called a taxi. 'You're on my way home,' he said, 'so I'll drop you off.'

'Thank you.'

When the taxi stopped, she looked wary. 'Would you, um…?' she began.

Yes, but he also knew it wouldn't be sensible and he needed time to get his head back in the right place. 'I've got some work to catch up on,' he fibbed. 'See you Sunday. It takes two and a half hours to get there; shall I pick you up at half-past eight?'

'I'll be ready,' she said.

He just hoped he managed to get his common sense back in place by Sunday. But he smiled and, once the light went on in her flat, he asked the cabbie to take him back to Islington.

On Sunday morning, Catriona was waiting outside her front door as Dominic pulled up to the kerb. He glanced at the clock on the dashboard: twenty-eight minutes past eight. He was early, but she'd been earlier.

'I hope you haven't been waiting long,' he said.

'Only about a minute,' she said.

'What's all that?' he asked, gesturing to the bags she was holding.

'Flowers for your mum, and a little thank-you for your sisters and Lou,' she said. 'And coffee for us.'

'You really didn't have to,' he said, 'but thank you. Mum and the girls will be pleased.' He stowed her bags safely in the car, then opened the passenger door for her. At her raised eyebrows, he said, 'This doesn't mean I think you're an incapable little woman, because you're nothing of the kind. It's how I was brought up. You open the door for your passenger.'

'Good manners rather than patronising works for me,' she said. 'Thank you.'

He climbed into the driver's side. 'Feel free to adjust the heating and put whatever you like on the radio.'

He wasn't surprised that she picked a classical music station; and he also wasn't surprised that she took refuge in her coffee to avoid talking.

But eventually she spoke. 'Dominic, I need to tell you something before we see your family.'

'Oh?'

She took a deep breath. 'This isn't the first time I've been engaged.'

Now that *did* surprise him. 'What happened?'

'I thought I'd learned from my parents' mistakes,' she said. 'Except I didn't. He thought a big flashy diamond ring gave him licence to cheat. I found out when I came home early from work, one afternoon. He was in bed—*my* bed—with someone I didn't know. I know everyone makes mistakes and you should give people a second chance, but it turned out that his affair had been going on for a while. And she wasn't the first. So I packed his things, made him give me my key back—and changed the locks. And then I moved.'

'I'm sorry he let you down so badly,' Dominic said.

'I let myself down,' she said. 'I should have seen through him. He was in love with the idea of marrying a viscount's granddaughter, of marrying into money. But he tried to make me feel it was my fault, for being cold.'

Her tone was even, but Dominic was starting to be able to read what she kept hidden. That accusation of coldness had really hurt her. Catriona wasn't cold, when you got to know her. She definitely used her intellect as a shield, but she *cared*.

'Now I get why you really didn't want a diamond engagement ring.' He frowned. 'Though, if your grandfather knew about this, that makes the clause inexcusable as well as even more un-explainable.'

'He didn't know the full story of why I broke

up with Luke,' Catriona said. 'Grannie was ill at the time. I didn't want to burden either of them.'

'That's hard,' Dominic said. 'But, even though this isn't the same kind of engagement, I can assure you I won't cheat on you. That's not who I am.'

'That's why I picked you as my convenient husband,' Catriona said with a glance at him.

'You know what you said about wanting to punch my father? That's how I feel about your ex, right now,' Dominic said.

'You might come off worse,' she warned. 'Luke was my personal trainer.'

So *that* was why she'd flinched about his sister's job. And why she preferred to walk in the park rather than train at the gym. Dominic's heart ached for her, though it wasn't from pity. It was something he couldn't define.

'I keep in shape. I'd rate my chances,' he said. 'Not all men are cheating scumbags, you know.'

'I know. I'm just disappointed that my judgement was so poor, given what my parents were like.' She wrinkled her nose. 'I'm sorry. I should've told you before.'

'No, but I'm glad you told me.' He paused. 'And it won't go any further than me.'

'Thank you,' she said.

Dominic's family were all there to greet them at his mother's house. To Catriona's surprise,

Ginny greeted her with a huge hug. She couldn't remember the last time anyone had done that, and it felt strange: as if the barriers she usually kept around herself were starting to melt.

'Oh, sweetheart, they're lovely,' Ginny said when Catriona gave her the flowers. 'Thank you.'

Dominic's sisters followed up with hugs, as did Tilly's husband Joe, Ginny's partner Ray and Suzy's partner Lou. Clearly Dominic's family were openly affectionate.

The girls allowed her enough time to have a coffee, then whisked her up to Suzy's room to try on the dresses.

All the ones she'd picked out were serviceable enough, but Suzy had added another. 'One of my friends designed this, and I think it's perfect for you.'

The dress was knee-length with a Bardot collar, in ivory silk; it was cinched in at the waist and had a flared skirt that fell to just below the knee. It wasn't the kind of style Catriona would have chosen, but Suzy had gone to a lot of effort, so she tried it on.

'That's definitely the one,' Tilly said.

Catriona stared at her reflection and felt as if her tongue was glued to her mouth.

'It's perfect,' Lou agreed.

And it was a million times better than the dress

Catriona had once dreamed of wearing on her wedding day.

Lou did a mock-up of her hair and make-up, and Ginny came in to give the final verdict. She stood in the doorway, looking stunned. 'Catriona, you look absolutely amazing! I want to hug you—but I don't want to spoil the dress.'

'Give us ten minutes, and she'll be back to normal and you can hug her,' Lou said.

After that they ran through the flowers and the wedding breakfast.

'Have you ordered a wedding cake?' Suzy asked.

'I wasn't going to bother,' Catriona said. 'Dominic's not a fan of cakes or puddings, and it's a small wedding.' She smiled at Ginny. 'Can I help you with lunch, Ginny?'

'All done. Sit down and have a glass of bubbles,' Ginny said. 'Dommy, there's a bottle in the fridge, if you could go and open it for us.'

'Sure,' he said with a smile.

'I…um…wanted to say thanks for your help,' Catriona said, and quietly dished out the gift bags she'd brought with her.

'You didn't need to do that! But thank you,' Tilly said, looking pleased.

'Can we open them now?' Suzy asked. At Catriona's nod, she did so. 'Oh, wow. This is seriously posh stuff. Thank you so much.' She pulled her in for another hug.

Catriona realised she was going to have to get used to the hugs. Dominic's family were all seriously tactile. 'You're welcome,' she said. 'You've all put a lot of work into helping us, and I appreciate it.' She felt the colour rise in her cheeks. 'Though I realise it's because of Dominic.'

'Now we're getting to know you,' Tilly said, 'it's for you as well.'

Catriona couldn't remember the last time she'd taken part in family Sunday lunch with any more people than her grandparents and Mrs MacFarlane; but she found herself really enjoying it. Even when Dominic's uncles and aunts arrived unexpectedly.

'I know you wanted to get to know Dominic's young lady properly and we were supposed to butt out,' one of his uncles said, 'but how could we pass up the chance to meet her? I'm Bill.'

'Of the guitar fame,' Catriona said.

Bill looked pleased. 'Dommy talks about my music?'

'I told you we'd fill you in later. *Don't* scare her away,' Ginny admonished. 'Catriona, this is my sister Shirl and her husband Bill, my sister Di and her husband Andy, and my sister Angie and her husband Glenn.'

'Who'd've thought it? Our little Dommy, getting married at last,' Shirl cooed.

'We've waited for *years* for him to bring a girl home,' Di added.

'Stop it, you two. You'll make the poor boy blush,' Angie said. 'But come here, Catriona, and let's give you a welcome hug.'

It sounded as if Dominic's aunts and uncles all thought the wedding was a real one.

'Go with it,' Dominic murmured in her ear. 'Think of it as a trial run for convincing your half-brothers.'

'How did you meet?' Angie asked, giving her a hug.

'We work together,' Catriona said.

'Love among all the legal fine print,' Shirl said with a grin.

'And the wedding's next month?' Di gave a very pointed look at Catriona's stomach.

'It's not a shotgun wedding, Auntie Di,' Dominic said, rolling his eyes. 'We just…didn't want to wait.'

'So what are you having as the first dance?' Bill asked.

'No dancing. We're driving to Scotland almost straight after wedding,' Dominic said.

'Which bit of Scotland?' Glenn asked.

'Roughly east-south-east of Edinburgh,' Catriona said.

'If you leave London at three, you'll be lucky to get there by eleven, even without any hold-ups,'

Bill said. 'You might be better off going the next day and doing more of the journey in daylight.'

'And that means you'll be able to have a couple of glasses of champagne with us to toast your wedding, instead of just a sip to keep you under the limit for driving,' Shirley said.

'It's going to be a very small wedding, Auntie Shirl,' Dominic said gently, 'given that Catriona recently lost her grandfather. Just Mum, the girls and their partners.'

Shirley bit her lip. 'Oh, love, I'm so sorry.' She gave Catriona a hug. 'You were close to him?'

'Yes,' Catriona said. Although it wasn't anything like the closeness Dominic had with his family, it wasn't a complete fib; she'd been closer to her grandfather and her grandmother than to anyone else in her family.

'Raise a glass to him on the day, love,' Bill said kindly. 'He'll know.'

'Yes.' She barely managed to get the word past the lump in her throat.

'I didn't mean to make you sad, love. Come on, we'll do a family sing,' Bill said.

'Bill,' Ginny said warningly.

'No, Gin, music's just the thing when you're feeling low,' he said. 'Back in a tick. I'll just nip out to the car.'

He returned without the guitar Catriona was expecting.

Catriona blinked as he checked the tuning of the instrument. 'Is that a *ukulele*?'

'It's easier to carry around than a guitar,' Bill said. 'You're a music fan?'

'Classical, mainly,' Catriona said.

'Ah.' Bill smiled, and played a piece that Catriona recognised instantly.

'The Prelude from Bach's cello suite,' she said. 'That's lovely. Thank you.'

The next thing she knew, he'd switched into a Beatles medley and everyone was singing along. She was shocked to find herself joining in when he segued into the Abba songs that everyone knew.

Dominic put an arm round her shoulders, squeezed her briefly and dropped a kiss on her hair. She knew he was doing it for show, to convince his aunts and uncles that this was a real courtship, but the sudden longing for contact was too much for her and she slid her arm round his waist. She felt him tense in surprise, and then he shifted just that little bit closer. And she could almost believe that he was singing some of the words of the songs to her. That this was going to be a real marriage, not a fake.

All too soon it was time to go back to London.

'Your family's lovely,' Catriona said when they were back on the motorway. 'You're so lucky to have grown up with all that...' The word 'love' caught in her throat.

'We have each other's backs,' he agreed. 'We're all out in force in the front row when Bill's band is playing, getting everyone dancing and singing. Aunty Shirl's a teacher, so when they do the summer fundraising fair we all donate raffle prizes and help man the stalls. Anyone needs a hand, we're there.'

What would it be like if her half-brothers did that? If they came and helped her with Lark Hill? But it was pointless wishing because she knew it wasn't going to happen.

'Your aunts and uncles are so disappointed about being left out of your wedding,' she said. 'I feel really guilty.'

'They understand it's a quiet wedding.'

And it wasn't a real one, she thought, so it shouldn't matter. Besides, what was the point of wishing for a real family wedding when they weren't actually going to be her family? It would only make it harder when she and Dominic had their quiet, amicable divorce and he walked away. She couldn't afford to get close to them.

'I've been thinking,' she said. 'Maybe your uncle's right about the drive. It isn't fair to Mrs MacFarlane, making her wait up and worry about us. We'd be better off going to Lark Hill the day after the wedding.'

He shot her a sidelong glance. 'Is this your way of telling me you're planning to go back to work, after the wedding? Except you can't, because you'll be on sabbatical. You're clearing your desk out, the evening before. Not that you have a lot to clear out.'

'It's inefficient to have clutter everywhere,' she said. Though she knew what he meant. She was about the only person in the office who had nothing personal on her desk, not even a pot plant. It had never bothered her before, but now she started to wonder if she was seriously out of step with the rest of the office—and the rest of the human race.

'I notice my sisters have given you a nickname,' he said.

She nodded. 'Trina.' At first, she'd found it strange; then she'd seen the affection behind it, and she secretly liked it.

'It sounds softer if you drop the first syllable of your name,' he mused. '"Trina" sounds like a girl who has fun. "Catriona" is the serious, scary lawyer.'

Precisely why she'd never admit to it in the office. But it still made her smile—as well as reminding her of his own nickname in the family. 'Like the difference between Dominic the London lawyer and "Dommy" who kicks a ball around in the park with all the family kids?'

'Something like that. So who are you in Scotland?' he asked.

'Just me,' she said.

'The Viscountess of Linton.'

'I'm still not used to the title,' she said. 'I intend to be on first-name terms with the tenants. Most of them have known me since I was tiny anyway.'

'If you're still just you,' he said thoughtfully, 'then you're fair, honest and hard-working.'

'Like Gramps,' she said.

He reached over to squeeze her hand briefly. 'You'll do a great job. And you'll bring something of you to the role, too.'

Except she didn't do personal. She kept everything brisk and businesslike. She'd prided herself on being professional; now, she was starting to wonder if that was enough.

When Dominic parked by her house, Catriona asked, 'Would you like to come in for a coffee?'

He was pretty sure she'd only invited him out of politeness, but he was intrigued to see what her flat was like. If it gave him any more clues as to who she really was. 'Thanks. That'd be lovely.'

Her flat was in a four-storey Georgian terrace; the houses had pale yellow bricks, tall, white-painted sash windows, and glossy black front doors with a rectangular fanlight above.

'Most of the houses are divided into flats,' she said as she unlocked her front door. 'I'm on the top two floors.'

He followed her up the stairs to her flat, where she let him into the black-and-white-tiled hall-way.

'It's a bit of an upside-down house,' she said. 'The bedrooms are on this floor.' She indicated one of the doors. 'That's the bathroom. Come up.'

There was another landing at the top of the stairs, and a black-and-white-tiled corridor. 'Living room,' she said, gesturing to one door, 'my office, and the kitchen. Would you prefer tea or coffee?'

'Coffee, please,' he said.

He followed her into the kitchen; the kitchen units were glossy cream, teamed with pale wood countertops and terracotta tiled flooring. A single door led to what he assumed was the terrace. There was a pale square wooden table with four chairs tucked neatly round it. Everything was incredibly tidy, and the only things on any of the work surfaces were the kettle and an expensive-looking coffee machine.

'That's a bean-to-cup machine, isn't it?' he asked.

'Because I don't want to put pods into land-fill,' she said. 'Besides, this way I get to choose my blend.' She gestured towards the living room. 'Take a seat,' she said, 'and I'll bring your cof-fee through.'

As he'd half-expected, her living room was organised and uncluttered, just like her clear desk policy at work, and it told him almost nothing about her. The room contained two small plain olive-green sofas with a small square coffee table next to each, and a sideboard which had a single brass lamp with a glass shade on top of it. It felt more like a show flat rather than a home.

The built-in bookshelves on either side of the chimney breast contained legal textbooks, historical novels and a few volumes about Tudor history; they were all shelved in strict alphabetical order by author surname, he noticed, and although he didn't recognise many of the names it was a fair bet that each author's novels were shelved in chronological order. It was clear that Catriona liked things orderly.

There was an antique carriage clock on the mantelpiece; it sat next to a silver photograph frame, which held a photo of Catriona at graduation with what he presumed were her grandparents. They were all smiling, but there was definitely an air of reserve about her grandparents: so very different to his own family. He remembered his own graduation, celebrating with his entire family. He had a feeling that Catriona's graduation celebrations had been an awful lot quieter.

There were no cushions or throws or any of the soft touches his mother, sisters and aunts had in their homes. There was a gilt mirror above the mantelpiece, a standard lamp by one of the sofas that was clearly used as a reading lamp, and the single piece of art on the walls was a small gilt-framed oil painting of a castle overlooking the sea. He wondered whether it was Lark Hill.

He couldn't resist peeking through the heavy brocade curtains; outside, there was a row of Georgian houses, and behind that he could see the greenery of Regent's Park—or what would look green on a spring morning rather than a winter night.

Catriona came in and handed him a mug of coffee, then took two coasters from a drawer in the sideboard and set one on each table. He had to hide a smile, because he knew she kept a coaster in her desk drawer at work, too. Was this how posh people lived, with everything kept hidden away?

The coffee was excellent, but he wasn't surprised—or that she was drinking what looked like chamomile tea. Her painted hoardings were very much back up, and he was beginning to think there was a layer of steel and barbed wire underneath. What would it take to persuade Catriona to let anyone close—to let *him* close? he wondered.

'It's a lovely flat,' he said.

'Thank you. I like it. It's a quiet road and it's

near the park.' She looked at him. 'I moved here seven years ago.'

He remembered she'd said that she'd moved after she'd discovered her fiancé's infidelity. Not wanting to dwell on tough memories for her, he changed the subject. 'Is that Lark Hill?' he asked, gesturing to the painting.

'Yes. Gramps commissioned it from a local artist when I was born, and my grandparents gave it to me for my twenty-fifth,' she said.

'And they're the ones with you in your graduation photo?'

She nodded. 'I probably should've asked my mother, but you could only have two guests and my grandparents were the ones who sent me weekly letters and chocolate when I was a student. I thought they'd enjoy it more than she would. And it was a lovely day. Sunny, bright, Oxford at its prettiest.'

If he'd studied away from home, his mother would've sent him a care package every week. It sounded as though Catriona's mother had clearly decided that giving birth was the limit of her familial duties, and had practically abandoned her daughter afterwards. No wonder Catriona was so aloof. 'My graduation was on a sunny day, too. Mum and Ray came to the ceremony—there was a limit of two tickets per graduand, but everyone else was waiting outside for me and they took a gazillion photos.' He laughed. 'Everyone took turns wearing my mortar board and having their photo taken with me. We spent the rest of the day celebrating, and it was good to share the day with them all.' He winced. 'Sorry. I know family stuff isn't the same for you.'

'It is what it is,' she said with a shrug. 'I've come to terms with it.'

Dominic wasn't quite so sure. There was something wistful in her eyes. He finished his coffee. 'Can I wash this up?' he asked, indicating his mug.

'No, it's fine,' she said, and took the mug from him.

'Guess I'll see you tomorrow, then,' he said, following her into the hallway.

She put the mugs on the kitchen worktop, then headed down the stairs to the front door.

He leaned forward and kissed her on the cheek. Her eyes went wide, and there was a distinct slash of colour across her cheekbones. Maybe she wasn't quite as immune to this thing between them as she acted.

'If we're going to convince your brothers that the wedding isn't a fake,' he said, 'we need to be comfortable with each other.'

'True.' But she didn't make a move towards him.

What he really wanted was for it to be like it had been on the boat, when she'd loosened her guard and kissed him. Though that in itself was scary, telling him that he was already getting too close to her. All the same, he kissed her other cheek, just to make the point. And then it was oh, so easy just to angle his face slightly and kiss the corner of her mouth. To move closer and tease her lips with his, tiny nibbling kisses intended to provoke her. And he thoroughly enjoyed the moment when she snapped, slid her arms round his neck, and pulled him closer. He let her set the place, and his pulse rocketed when she deepened the kiss.

This wasn't his imagination.

There was a definite spark between them. A spark he would never have known existed if she hadn't suggested the wedding deal. But now he knew—and he wanted more.

She pulled back. 'Comfortable enough for you?' she drawled.

Was she saying that kiss had all been an act? That she'd played him, the way he'd kind of tried to play her? 'Maybe,' he said, affecting a coolness he definitely didn't feel. 'It's a start.'

'Goodnight, Dominic. See you in the office.' Though, despite the calmness of her tone, he could see the glitter in her eyes. That kiss had affected her as much as it had affected him.

The question was: what were they going to do about it?

CHAPTER SEVEN

DOMINIC BROODED ABOUT it all the way home. It was a dilemma he couldn't really discuss with anyone.

Where did you take your fiancée-who-wasn't-really on a date-that-wasn't-really, on the grounds of getting to know each other better so they could look relaxed when they stood next to each other at *their* wedding, instead of as if they were scared the other might accidentally scald them? Especially when you discovered that actually, you were really attracted to your fake bride-to-be and you thought she might feel the same about you?

This was bizarre. He'd never been in a position before where he didn't have a clue where to take his date. But Catriona was so guarded and self-contained that he couldn't work out what sort of thing she might like.

Checking the internet didn't help. The 'first date' ideas in winter were all just too samey. Going to glitzy, Instagrammable bars; wrapping up warm for a walk in the park and then having hot chocolate together; a winter brunch.

What he needed was something that would make them have to get close and physical.

Dancing? Except Catriona preferred classical music, which pretty much ruled out a nightclub.

He couldn't imagine her ice-skating at any of the seasonal pop-up rinks, either.

She'd grown up in a castle and she read historical novels. Maybe he could take her to a museum? Except their visit would need to be outside office hours, which in most cases would mean a weekend. He was pretty sure she'd like something like the Queen's House at Greenwich, with its amazing staircase, or maybe something more unusual, like the Petrie Museum of Egyptian Archaeology.

Maybe he should just ask her what she'd like to do.

Considering their office was open plan and she was only a few feet away…everyone would hear their conversation. So he'd do it a more subtle way.

Assuming that, like him, she turned her phone to silent when she was at work, he texted her.

Yo, Fifi. You busy at the weekend?

Why? was the answer.

Typical Catriona, giving nothing away.

Wondered if you wanted to go to the Queen's House in Greenwich. Or a museum. Would suggest this evening but can't find any open late. Maybe British Museum on Friday's late opening?

Either would be nice.

Cinema tonight? Maybe we could go to one of the live theatre screenings, if there's one on.

Sounds good. Let me know what time.

He checked the listings, found one at a cinema the other side of Regent's Park from her flat, and booked their tickets, then texted her the details.

Film starts at seven.

Thank you, Fergus.

That cheekiness in her reply made him smile. Then:

This is the cinema chain that delivers food and drink to your seat, yes? If so, I'll buy drinks and food.

Perfect. Meet you outside Baker Street tube station after work?

It was only a couple of stops on the Circle line from St Pancras to Baker Street; he left the office first, and waited for her outside the tube station entrance. She'd clearly caught the train after his, because she was only five minutes behind him.

'This was a really nice idea,' she said. 'I haven't been to the cinema for ages.'

'Me, neither.' He paused. 'I thought if we spent some time together, we'd get used to each other and we won't look awkward in the wedding photos.'

'That's a good idea,' she said. 'And this is the cinema, so I guess maybe we could hold hands through the film?'

'Or, as we have a sofa, put our arms round each other?' he suggested. 'Then perhaps we can go for a drink and discuss the film afterwards.'

'That works for me,' she said. There was a tinge of colour in her cheeks which Dominic found endearing. Strange how someone who was so confident in her job was so awkward when it came to anything close and personal.

He took her hand and they headed for the cinema. They ordered pizza and a glass of red wine each, found their seats on one of the plush sofas, then made themselves comfortable.

Once they'd eaten their pizza and the film had started, he slid his arm round her shoulders. She stayed absolutely rigid against him at first, but gradually she nestled in closer and eventually rested her head on his shoulder. Dominic was very aware of her warmth against him, and how long it had been since he'd last sat like this with one of his dates. He had a feeling it was even longer for Catriona.

Sitting here with her in semi-darkness, watching a performance by actors at the top of their game, was hugely enjoyable. And he liked the fact that Catriona seemed to be relaxing with him at last.

At the end of the film, they headed for one of the nearby wine bars. Because it was a Monday evening, it was relatively quiet and Dominic really enjoyed discussing the performance with her.

Eventually the bar staff announced last orders.

He stared at her in shock. 'How did that happen? Sorry. I didn't mean to keep you out so late.'

'I enjoyed it,' she said. 'Maybe we can do this again.'

'I'd like that, too,' he said. He glanced at the window. 'It's raining. I'll call us a cab and drop you off on the way back to mine.'

'But I'm not on your way.'

'You are, if we take the scenic route,' he said with a smile. He booked a taxi on his phone app, and kissed her goodnight when the cab pulled up outside her flat. 'We'll wait here until your living room light comes on,' he said. 'So I know you're in safely.'

Even though she lived in a very safe area, Catriona appreciated the way Dominic was looking out for her. Luke certainly hadn't cherished her like this, and he'd been her real fiancé, not her fake one.

And she found herself really aware of whenever Dominic was sitting at his desk in the office. He caught her eye across the room several times during the week, though she was relieved he didn't suggest having lunch together, because she didn't want the rest of the team to know that she was sort-of dating him. Or, worse, why she was doing it.

But they had dinner out in Covent Garden on Thursday night, and she enjoyed walking hand in hand with him around the piazza, taking in the lights and the music and the people.

'One for the dossier. Ballet—yes or no?' she asked as they walked past the Royal Opera House.

'I've never been,' he said. 'But I'm guessing the music means you like it?'

She nodded. 'The music, the movement and the costumes. And I had ballet classes when I was small.'

'I've always thought of ballet as being for posh people,' he said.

She grinned. 'Would you be stereotyping me there, Fergus?'

'I don't know any other viscountesses to compare you with, Fifi,' he said. 'But, if you like ballet, then I'd be happy to go to a performance with you.'

'All right. I'll get us tickets to *The Nutcracker*,' she said.

'And maybe you'd like to come to a blues night with me?'

'If you can step outside your comfort zone,' she said, 'I can step outside mine. Just let me know the dress code.'

'Whatever you're comfortable wearing,' he said. 'Is there a dress code for ballet?'

'Tutu?' she suggested.

'Is that a dare?' His eyes sparkled wickedly, and she knew he'd do it.

'That would almost be worth signing up for social media, to get a picture of you in a tutu,' she said with a grin.

'I could handle the office,' he said, 'but not my sisters. Will my office suit do?'

'Yes.' He looked seriously good in a suit.

He leaned close enough to whisper, 'But you could always wear a tutu for me. A private dance.'

'It's years since I did a class. I don't even have shoes, let alone a leotard and tutu.'

'You could improvise.' He nibbled her earlobe and, despite the coolness of the night air, she suddenly felt hot all over. Because now she could imagine herself in an intimate setting with Dominic. Candlelight. Dancing for him in a chiffon skirt…

'Whatever just put that expression on your face,' he said, 'I'd love to know.'

She blushed furiously, but didn't dare share it, because she was rapidly getting out of her depth. 'Ballet tickets,' she said instead, knowing that she was chickening out. 'Any particular night—except Wednesdays, obviously, because that's reserved for your family?'

'Any night except Wednesdays,' he said.

On Saturday, they visited the Queen's House, and Dominic took a photograph of Catriona sitting on the famous Tulip Staircase.

'You know they're really fleurs-de-lys, not tulips?' she asked. 'So it ought to be the Lily Staircase.'

'And they're not really painted blue—it's smalt, made from pondered cobalt glass,' he said. 'It's the first geometric self-supporting spiral staircase built in England.'

She grinned. 'You looked it up before we came here, too.'

'Of course. I can't have you being better-informed than me,' he said.

'Oh, now that sounds like a challenge,' she teased, enjoying the sparkle in his eyes.

'How to out-nerd a nerd. You're on.'

She raised an eyebrow. 'You're calling me a nerd?'

'It takes one to know one,' he said, and kissed her lightly. 'My nerdiness just happens to be in different areas.'

Yet they *fitted*. And part of Catriona was starting to wish that this was real, instead of being part of their project of getting used to each other so the wedding photographs would look authentic. That they were a real couple, wandering through an ancient house with their arms round each other.

Over the next three weeks, they spent more time together. After the ballet, Dominic admitted that he was surprised by how much he'd enjoyed the performance and wouldn't mind seeing more. And at the blues club, Catriona was surprised to discover that she really liked eating hot quesadillas and drinking cold beer with him, and then watching the show from the front row, with Dominic standing behind her with his arms wrapped round her, swaying in time to the music.

He was doing so much for her. She wanted to do something special for him, and a bit of sleuthing on the internet found her the perfect thing. She booked it for the Friday evening before the wedding and managed to keep it secret from him; the only thing she'd tell him was that he needed to meet her at her flat at quarter to seven, wearing a long-sleeved T-shirt, trainers and tracksuit bottoms—but not baggy ones.

'Are we doing a workout together, or something?' he asked when she opened the door. 'Because I thought…'

That she didn't do the gym, after Luke. She appreciated the fact that he didn't rub it in her face. 'It's an "or something",' she said, closing the front door behind her.

He narrowed his eyes at her. 'Where are we going?'

'For roughly a ten-minute walk. And we'll come back here to eat, afterwards. Stop asking questions,' she said.

When he persisted with the questions, she stopped dead. When he turned to her, she stood on tiptoe, slid her arms round his neck, and kissed him.

It silenced him for about five minutes.

'Workout clothes,' he said as she led him along the street. 'You're not taking me to a ballet class?'

She laughed. 'No tutus involved. Not even a dance belt and tights for you,' she said.

'How disappointing, Fifi.' A little later, he suggested, 'Trampolining?'

She almost told him he was getting warmer, but she didn't want to spoil the surprise. 'Not trampolining.'

'But it must be some sort of workout. Fencing?'

'No.'

'Kick-boxing?'

'No.'

He went quiet, and she could practically see the cogs turning in his head.

But finally he seemed to realise that she wasn't going to be drawn, and the questions subsided.

'I promise you'll like it,' she said.

'Boxing?'

'No. Nothing you'd do in a gym.'

'I give up,' he said.

'Good. Just through here.' She ushered him into the foyer of a community centre. And she was thrilled that she actually made his jaw drop when she introduced him to the woman who was giving them a special taster session in trapeze skills.

'You remembered what I told you about when I was eight,' he said. 'How long have you been planning this?'

'Ages,' she said.

He wrapped his arms round her. 'You're amazing,' he said softly. 'Thank you. And you're doing it with me?'

'I'm absolutely terrified,' she said, 'but, yes, I'm doing it with you.'

'The static trapeze isn't as scary as a flying trapeze,' Celeste told her. 'What I'm going to do is teach you both the basics, and then we're going to put together a small routine to music. It'll only be about a minute, but it'll be fun.'

'What if I fall off?' Catriona asked, thinking of how much a fracture would potentially hamper her.

'That's why there are crash mats underneath the trapeze,' Celeste said with a smile. 'Several of them, two deep. But people don't tend to fall off. You'll be fine.'

Celeste took them through a warm-up, then showed them how to get up on the trapeze. Dominic went first, and Catriona was amazed by how gracefully he moved. He looked slightly nervous when Celeste encouraged him to stand on the bar, but then a wide smile crossed his face.

'It's even better than I dreamed it would be,' he said when he'd dismounted and it was Catriona's turn. 'I can't believe you did this for me.'

'I wanted you to have some fun,' she said.

'And how.' He stole a kiss. 'I might run away from the office to do more of this…'

Catriona gripped the ropes very tightly, but managed to point her feet the way Celeste encouraged her to. 'It's like ballet, except in the air,' Celeste said. 'Think of the shapes.'

Dominic caught her eye. *Tutu*, he mouthed, and she couldn't help grinning back.

They changed places every few minutes, taking turns on the trapeze. By the third go, Catriona found herself relaxing, but Dominic was clearly in his element.

Finally, Celeste put on some music Catriona recognised.

'It's the waltz from Shostakovich's *Jazz Suite*,' she said.

'This one always makes me think of the trapeze,' Celeste said. 'And we're going to put everything you've learned together.'

'Is it OK if I film Dommy's routine, to show his mum and sisters?' Catriona asked.

Celeste gestured to Dominic. 'Your call, sweetie.'

'Sure,' he said, but there was something unreadable in his expression.

She filmed him getting onto the bar, moving his body into a graceful horizonal arch before going upside down, getting back up on the bar and onto his feet, then wrapping himself round the rope on one side, sliding down to a sitting position, and doing a forward roll around the bar.

'That felt amazing,' he said, when he got back onto the floor.

'It looked pretty impressive from here, too,' she said.

'Thank you.' He smiled at her. 'Your turn to get up there and strut your stuff.'

She didn't feel as fluid as he'd looked, though the ballet classes she'd taken at school meant she was comfortable with the arms and pointing her feet, but she went through the routine.

'You were both fabulous,' Celeste said. 'Did you enjoy it?'

'It was incredible. Better than I dreamed it would be, when I was a kid,' Dominic said. 'I loved it. Do you do longer courses?'

'I do one that covers all the aerial skills,' Celeste said. 'Silks, hoops and ropes, plus the trapeze. I can give you the details.'

'Yes, please. I'd definitely like to do it,' Dominic said.

'I think I'd prefer to watch,' Catriona said with a smile. 'I enjoyed doing this tonight, but it's a little bit too far out of my comfort zone.'

They walked back to Catriona's flat, with Dominic's arm round her shoulders and hers round his waist.

'I'm blown away by what you did for me,'

Dominic said. 'I've always wanted to do that. And I only told you about it briefly.'

'You know my reputation. I pay attention to detail,' she said, though secretly she was thrilled that he'd liked her surprise so much.

'Details queen—no, make that empress,' he said. 'I'll be buzzing for a week after that.'

'I'm glad you enjoyed it. But I think I'm strictly sidelines for the scary stuff,' she said. 'Support crew, that's me.'

'You're amazing,' he said.

She was starting to think that about him, too. But she couldn't let herself get carried away. They'd be married on Tuesday, and then they'd be applying for divorce next Christmas. That was the deal, and she needed to remember that.

Back at her flat, she began cooking them a stir fry.

'I must be able to do something to help,' Dominic said.

'I bought everything ready-prepped,' she said. 'It's going to take five minutes of stirring.'

'Can I lay the table?'

'Already done.'

'Make you a cup of tea?'

'No.'

'Then I'll loiter,' he said, leaning against the doorframe with his arms crossed. 'You know, you called me "Dommy" tonight.'

'Did I?' She felt her eyes widen. 'Sorry. It slipped out.'

'I liked it when you called me that,' he said. 'Trina.'

'I'm not sure I like my name being shortened,' she muttered, to cover her confusion.

'It suits you, actually. Not the formal you, in the office, but the you outside. You're like a rose, with layers and layers until you get to that soft, sweet heart.'

One that didn't exist, according to Luke. 'I'm not soft and I'm not sweet. Lawyers aren't sweet!'

'Your painted hoardings,' he said, leaning forward to boop her nose, 'don't do you justice.'

Oh, help. If he carried on complimenting her like that, her knees would go weak. And she couldn't afford to let herself fall for him for real. 'Go and sit down. Dinner's nearly ready,' she said, ushering him out of the kitchen.

Something had changed between them. Something she couldn't define, but when he kissed her goodnight—under the usual excuse of it being to make them comfortable with each other for the wedding photographs—it felt like a real kiss. As if he meant it. Her blood fizzed as his mouth brushed hers, tempting and cajoling until she kissed him back.

She was going to have to be very, very careful.

***

It was the day before the wedding.

The day she left work. Officially on sabbatical for a year, to sort out some family business; but would she ever come back to the office?

Catriona pushed down her worries and made sure she'd handed over all her projects thoroughly. At the end of the day, she cleared out her desk and was about to slip out quietly when Lewis, the senior partner, came over. 'Can I see you for a minute in my office?' he said.

Was he going to tell her privately that he'd made Dominic the new partner, out of courtesy, because she'd been his rival? She couldn't think of any other reason for him to want a private word. 'Sure,' she said. 'So Dominic's getting his promotion?'

'In due course, my dear,' Lewis said with a smile.

But when he opened his door to usher her in, she realised that everyone in the firm was crowded into his office.

The second thing she noticed were the champagne flutes and bottles of champagne on his desk.

Maybe this wasn't going to be a private word, after all, but a public celebration of Dominic's success. And she was pleased for him—after all, she'd stepped down from the partnership race, and he was doing his side of the bargain tomorrow. Just…at the same time, part of her felt a bit wistful. This could've been her celebration, as the new partner.

But she'd made the deal with Dominic, and he deserved it, so she'd smile.

'I know you thought you were going to get away without any fuss, Catriona,' Lewis said, 'but we couldn't let you go without giving you a toast.'

What?

This wasn't about Dominic?

'We know you're coming back next year,' Sophie, one of the other partners, said. 'But you've been here a long time, and we wanted to wish you well in your sabbatical.' She handed over a large envelope which Catriona assumed held a card signed by everyone, plus a beautifully wrapped rectangular box.

'We hope you like it,' one of the others said.

She opened the box carefully to reveal a really gorgeous fountain pen.

'Thank you,' she said. 'It's lovely. And it's really kind of you all.' She hadn't expected this at all. Maybe a private, 'All the best and keep in touch' from the partners, but she knew she had a reputation for being driven and focused on her work, and she'd never really felt that her colleagues liked her. Respected her, yes; but that wasn't the same thing. She didn't have Dominic's easy charm. People would come to her for help with a knotty legal problem, but not for anything personal.

She thanked each of her colleagues individually, and somehow managed to make polite small talk until people started slipping away, and then quietly said her goodbyes. Dominic had already left, and she felt obscurely miserable on the way back to her flat.

Tomorrow was the wedding and the day after they were driving to Scotland; she'd decided which letting agency to use for her flat and which storage place for the things she wasn't taking to Scotland, and had planned to do that quietly after Christmas. There was nothing else to be done and, for the first time since she could remember, she was at a complete loss about what to do next.

She was about to resort to doing online word games—her secret vice—when her intercom buzzed.

Odd. She wasn't expecting a delivery or any visitors. 'Hello?' she said.

'Special delivery,' Dominic said. 'Can I come up?'

'Of course.' She buzzed him up, then opened her door.

'Hey. I thought you might be feeling a bit flat,'

he said as she let him in. 'I know I would be, in your shoes.'

'I've worked there for nearly seven years. It's a long time, and life's going to change a lot for me tomorrow. Well, except my name. That's not changing.'

'Indeed, my dear Viscountess of Linton,' he said dryly.

How did she tell him that she always felt as if she was on the outside, looking in? But she didn't want him to pity her, so she did what she always did and stuffed her feelings back down inside.

'Did you know about the leaving do?'

'Yes,' he said. 'They were having trouble thinking about what to get you.'

'The pen's lovely. Very thoughtful.'

But they both knew it was the kind of gift you'd get for someone you didn't really know—a pen was *safe*.

'I got you something else,' he said. He took a small velvet box from his pocket. 'As you wouldn't let me get you an engagement ring.'

Her eyes widened. 'But…'

'I hope you'll like it,' he said. 'I know you don't like flashy stuff.'

Her breath caught as she opened the box. It was a delicate pendant—and it was exactly like her grandmother's engagement ring, a ruby surrounded by old-cut diamonds so it looked like a daisy, on a narrow gold chain.

'That's beautiful,' she said. 'Dominic—I don't know what to say. I wasn't expecting anything. And this is just…'

It filled her with wonder that he'd read her so well. And she didn't know how to explain it, so she hoped he could see it in her eyes as she looked up at him.

'I'm glad I got it right,' he said, and smiled.

'I didn't buy you anything.'

'That's not how presents work, Catriona,' he said. 'I wasn't giving this to you in the expectation of receiving something. I thought you might like it, that's all. I wanted to give you something for *you*. Something pretty and understated.'

So unlike the flashy diamond Luke had bought.

This was perfect. The exact sort of thing she would've chosen for herself. It was the nicest thing that anyone had ever bought her.

'Would you help me put it on?' She handed the box back to him.

'Sure.'

He took the necklace from the box; she felt his fingers against the nape of her neck, and then the pendant hung at the perfect height against her skin.

'Come and see,' he said, and drew her over to the mantelpiece.

She stared at her reflection, then caught his gaze in the mirror. 'It's beautiful. Thank you.'

'You're very welcome,' he said. And then he spun her round to face him. Brushed his mouth lightly against hers.

This wasn't for show. It felt as if it was for real. And she wasn't sure whether she was more terrified or delighted.

He stepped back, his expression completely unreadable. 'I'll see you tomorrow at the register office,' he said. 'Goodnight.'

Part of her wanted to ask him to stay; but how could she do that? This thing between them was a business arrangement. Besides, even though it wasn't a real wedding, she was mindful of the old tradition that it was bad luck to see the groom on the day until she walked down the aisle. She'd never thought herself the superstitious sort, but she didn't want to take any risks.

'Goodnight,' she whispered, and she let him see himself out.

CHAPTER EIGHT

THE NEXT MORNING, Catriona woke early, feeling decidedly antsy. Partly because it wasn't a normal Tuesday, and she wouldn't be going to the office; and partly because it was her wedding day. A wedding that would save her childhood home—but would also make her life complicated, because the way she was starting to feel about Dominic Ferrars made her feel distinctly vulnerable.

Muffling herself in a thick coat and walking up Primrose Hill to watch the sunrise didn't make her feel any better.

Was this all a huge mistake? Should she have just let Lark Hill be sold and the money divided between the boys?

But Lark Hill wasn't about money. It was about the people who lived on the estate. The history. The responsibilities her father would've shirked. The responsibilities she needed to shoulder.

She could do this.

She *had* to do this.

She'd arranged for Dominic's mum, sisters and Lou to get changed at her flat before the wedding, and Dominic was hosting the men of the party and baby Aiden. They arrived at ten, with a flurry of bags and paraphernalia.

Ginny gave her a hug. 'I know this must be hard for you, love. I wish you'd got someone on your side coming to the wedding. It feels as if we're taking over.'

'It's not a real wedding,' Catriona reminded her. Even though part of her wished it could be, and she knew she was supposed to *look* like a bride today. Happy. Looking forward to the future with the man she loved. Counting the seconds until she walked down the aisle to him, hardly able to wait to say her vows.

They'd chosen the vows together. Something they could say with total honesty: *I promise to be faithful and loyal, to respect and cherish you, to support you through the good times and the bad.*

No false declarations of love.

But the words had resonated deep inside. If she were in a real relationship, it was exactly what she wanted. To be faithful and loyal, and know that her partner would do the same. To be respected and cherished, just as she would do to him. Support.

And she couldn't help but wonder: if you

added all those things together, wouldn't the sum be greater than the parts? With the added physical attraction between them—an attraction she definitely hadn't admitted to and neither had he—wouldn't that be *actual* love?

But she wasn't looking for love. She was looking to save the castle. And Dominic was helping her. They'd made a deal. A marriage of convenience, when his family deserved something real.

'And I'm sorry I'm depriving you of a real wedding. You're all so nice and you don't deserve this.' The words burst out of her, along with a tear she couldn't blink back in time.

Lou wiped away the tear that spilled over. 'Hey, it's bad luck to cry on your wedding day, even if it isn't a traditional one. Plus, it'll be harder for me to do your make-up if you're all blotchy.' She nudged Catriona. 'Give us a smile—that's better.'

'And anyway, today means we get to dress up a bit and see Dommy and have a nice lunch out with you, too—we're all fine with this,' Tilly said.

'But we all think your family seriously needs someone to shake some common sense into them,' Suzy said. 'The way they treat you is terrible.'

'Forget them. Today,' Ginny said, '*we're* your family.'

Catriona had a huge lump in her throat. 'Thank you. I, um, can I make you all some coffee? Or would you like bubbles? There's champagne in the fridge. A couple of bottles.'

Suzy gave her a hug. 'Bubbles are perfect. Dommy told us you're a cheese fiend, like him, so we brought crumpets and cheese with us because I bet you were too nervous to eat breakfast.'

'I was,' Catriona admitted.

'Do you mind me taking over your kitchen? I promise I'm not as messy as Dommy probably told you I am,' Suzy said.

'That's fine. I can't remember the last time I had crumpets,' Catriona said. 'Thank you.'

'You know, it's a shame this isn't a real wedding, because you fit right in with us,' Tilly said.

Nobody had ever said that to Catriona before, even her best friend, and she had to blink again.

'No tears!' Lou said. 'Let's get the bubbles open—and we need photos.'

'My job!' Suzy said, waving her phone. 'Say "crumpets and cheese".'

Finally, hair and make-up done, they all finished changing into their wedding outfits.

'You look amazing, Catriona,' Ginny said. 'Your grandparents would've been so proud.'

'It's all thanks to you all. If you'd left me to

it, Dominic and I would've just got married at lunchtime and gone back to work,' Catriona said.

'You deserve better than that,' Ginny said.

Then Catriona's phone pinged. 'Our taxi will be here in five minutes.'

It gave them just enough time to pack everything they needed to take with them, and then it was time to head for Camden Town Hall.

Dominic paced up and down outside Camden Town Hall. Ridiculous, he knew, but he felt as nervous as if this was the real thing.

What scared him even more was that Catriona could tempt him to *want* this to be real. But she was as self-contained as the rose he'd said she reminded him of, full of layers. Or maybe she was like a daisy, hiding away in the grass and not letting anyone really see her.

Except he thought he was beginning to see who she really was—and, the more he got to know her, the more he liked her.

'Their taxi's here,' Ray said. 'It's bad luck to see the bride. Go and wait for her in the room. Joe, Aiden and I will bring them all in.'

'OK,' Dominic said. Why was it that he felt as if this was his driving test and every single exam he'd ever sat, plus every job interview he'd done, all rolled into one?

The door to the room they'd booked was open.

He knocked on it, more out of courtesy than anything else, and walked in.

'Good afternoon, Mr Ferrars,' the registrar greeted him.

'Good afternoon,' he said. 'Everyone's here.'

'Don't worry. All grooms feel nervous, however small or large the wedding,' she said with a smile. 'We'll try to make this as easy as we can for you.'

A couple of minutes later, his mother walked down the aisle on Ray's arm and took her seat, followed by Tilly, Joe and Aiden, and then Suzy and Lou.

'You look gorgeous,' Suzy said. 'And I'm glad you listened to me and wore the bow tie to match your buttonhole.'

'You look gorgeous, too,' he said. 'All of you.'

Then Catriona walked into the room and every word vanished out of his head. She looked stunning, in a knee-length ivory dress with a cinched waist and a Bardot neckline, baring her shoulders. She was carrying a bunch of white gerberas, the stems taped together and the heads in a ball, softened with gypsophila and accented with eryngium like the one he wore as a buttonhole. There was a headdress of pearls and crystals wound through her short hair, rather than a veil. She wore her usual pearl earrings, but he noticed that she was wearing his ruby-and-diamond pendant.

And she was walking down the aisle to him.

It wasn't a real wedding. Of course it wasn't. They were both clear on that.

But it felt like one, and he couldn't shift that feeling.

'You look amazing,' he whispered as she came to stand beside him.

'So do you,' she whispered back, an almost shy blush tinging her cheeks.

Again, the unexpected feelings slammed into him. *She thought he looked amazing, too. She'd gone all shy when he'd told her his own reaction.*

The registrar took them through the ceremony, and he could barely pay attention because he was so focused on the woman standing next to him.

Then they came to the legal bit.

'I declare that I know of no legal reason why I, Dominic Ferrars, may not be joined in marriage to Catriona Findlay,' he said.

Catriona echoed his declaration.

And then it was the contracting words. 'I, Dominic Ferrars, take you, Catriona Findlay, to be my wedded wife,' he said.

'I, Catriona Findlay, take you, Dominic Ferrars, to be my wedded husband,' she answered.

Rings. Where the hell had he put the rings? He rummaged in his pocket, panicking slightly that he'd messed this up and it was all going wrong; but then Joe stepped forward and handed him a small velvet bag. Dominic tipped the two plain gold rings into his hand and slid one onto the ring finger of Catriona's left hand. 'I give you this ring as a symbol of our marriage,' he said. 'I promise to be faithful and loyal, to respect and cherish you, to support you through the good times and the bad.'

Words they'd chosen together which had deliberately not included the L-word. At the same time they were vows he would stand by. Vows he believed in. Faithfulness was a definite, given her background. He'd be loyal to her, and he knew she'd be the same towards him. They respected each other. They'd support each other through the good times and the bad.

The sticky bit was cherishing.

Would she let him cherish her? Or would it make her back away?

She took the other ring, and he could feel her fingers trembling slightly as she slid the ring onto his finger and repeated his vow.

There was definite trepidation in her eyes, too. She was nervous, clearly feeling as mixed-up about this as he did. They'd stick to their bargain; that wasn't in doubt. He had the partnership and she had the castle.

But cherishing.

The more he'd got to know Catriona, the more he liked her. And it made him antsy, because he hadn't ever felt like that towards anyone he'd dated. She'd once been engaged for real and been let down; it was one of the reasons why she didn't let anyone close. But would their marriage of convenience change things?

Because being convenient didn't necessarily mean their marriage couldn't be real…

'I'm delighted to pronounce you husband and wife,' the registrar said. 'Congratulations. Now I'd like you and your witnesses to sign the register.'

He signed his name: *Dominic Ferrars*.

Catriona's eyes crinkled very slightly at the corners, and she signed *Catriona Findlay*.

'I'd like to introduce the newlyweds, Dominic Ferrars and Catriona Findlay,' the registrar declared.

If this had been a real wedding, Dominic wouldn't have insisted that she changed her name. He'd want her for who she was: Catriona Findlay, his clever rival with her eye for detail and refusal to compromise.

'You're meant to kiss the bride, now, Dommy,' Tilly called.

Catriona gave him the very tiniest nod, and he kissed her. Her mouth felt soft and sweet and full of promise as it moved against his, and he had to stop himself pulling her closer and kissing her harder.

On the steps outside, they paused for wedding photos, and Suzy and Tilly scattered the white delphinium petals Catriona had chosen as confetti. 'And now for a very traditional bit,' Catriona said, and threw her bouquet straight at Lou, who caught it and grinned back.

Suzy kissed her girlfriend and said, 'I think that might just be a sign,' and everyone laughed.

The hotel was literally a two-minute walk away, so they cut through the streets; people smiled at the wedding party, wishing them well.

Catriona had managed to book a small private dining room; lunch was beautifully presented and tasted even better.

'What happened to the speeches?' Tilly asked when the hotel staff had cleared everything away.

Dominic and Catriona looked at each other. 'I think we can dispense with speeches,' Catriona said. 'It's not exactly a traditional wedding.'

'Well, there's one tradition we can't dispense with,' Ginny said, and gave a signal to the waiter.

'Mum?' Dominic asked.

And then the waiter brought in a platter covered with a silver dome.

'This is from Di,' Ginny said. 'She knows it's only a small wedding and our Dommy's weird about puddings, but she didn't want everyone else to be deprived of cake.'

'Auntie Di makes all the family cakes,' Tilly confided to Catriona. 'And they always taste as amazing as they look.'

Family. They were including her, Dominic thought. He glanced swiftly at her, wondering if his family's enthusiasm would all be too much; but there was a softness to her smile that made him think she was relaxed, even enjoying it.

The waiter lifted the dome to reveal a small cake, beautifully decorated with gerbera and eryngium.

'We showed her the wedding flowers, and she made them out of sugar,' Suzy said.

'I'm stunned. That's so lovely,' Catriona said. 'We'll send her flowers to say thank you.'

'That's sweet of you—but what she really wants,' Ginny said, 'is for us to video you two cutting the cake.' She gave them both a speaking look. 'Cutting the cake, and kissing.'

'We can do that,' Dominic said.

'Of course we can do that,' Catriona said.

She wanted him to kiss her?

Or was she trying to play a part, trying to make this look real to convince her family?

He and Catriona posed for a photograph, with the cake, and then the waiter gave them a silver knife to cut it.

'Videoing in three, two, one—*now*,' Ginny said, holding up her phone.

They cut the cake, and Dominic kissed her lightly. Though, weirdly, it made all the blood in his veins feel as if it were fizzing.

'Thank you for the cake, Auntie Di,' he said to the camera.

'It's the most beautiful cake I've ever seen—it matches our flowers perfectly,' Catriona added. 'Thank you.'

It tasted as good as it looked; even Dominic, who normally wasn't keen on sweet stuff, liked his aunt's cakes.

'This is where I wish Bill had managed to teach me to play the ukulele, so I could've played a first dance for you,' Ray said.

'Way ahead of you,' Tilly said. 'We also need some first dance pics. And Bill recorded something specially for you.'

That was going too far. He needed to stop this before Catriona backed away. 'We don't have time. You'll be late for your train,' Dominic said.

'No, we won't. We can spare four minutes,' Tilly said. 'Mum—you're in charge of the camera.' She gestured to Dominic and Catriona. 'You got away without speeches, but you *don't* get away without a first dance.'

'We're under orders,' Dominic said, and held out a hand to Catriona.

'I can't remember the last time I danced,' she said, but to his relief she took his hand.

'Guess you'll just have to trust me to lead,' he said, 'though I have no idea what Bill might be thinking.' Unable to resist the idea of dancing with her any more, he spun her into his arms.

Tilly pressed 'play' on her phone, and the first chords of 'Moondance' floated into the air, played on an electro-acoustic guitar.

The perfect song. He smiled and drew her close. 'Your dress is perfect for this,' he whispered. And he couldn't help adding, '*You're* perfect for this.'

The first dance. *Their wedding dance.* And the way Dominic danced with her to the song, a slow and sensual sway, made Catriona feel giddy. He spun her out and then back into his arms, making the skirt of her dress flare out. And then, when the song ended, he bent her back over his arm theatrically, and pulled her back up again before kissing her.

She forgot about their wedding guests. As far as she was concerned, nobody else was in the room. All she could think of was the touch of his mouth against hers. The feel of his heart thudding against hers. The warmth of his skin. How much she wanted him…

When he broke the kiss, he looked as dazed as she felt.

'And that's a wrap. I think Uncle Bill's going to forgive you for not letting him play at your wedding,' Suzy said.

Just for show. This was just for show, Catriona reminded herself. But, so far, their wedding day had felt very real indeed. Something that scared and thrilled her in equal measure: because who knew where this might lead?

'But you're right—we do need to make a move for the train,' Ginny said. 'But we'll send you pictures and videos soon.'

With almost military efficiency, Dominic's family got themselves ready for travelling. Catriona and Dominic went next door to the station with them, to wave them off.

Ginny hugged Catriona hard before they went through the barriers. 'You're one of us now,' she whispered. 'I don't care if this isn't a real wedding and you're not changing your surname to Dommy's, you're *still* one of us.'

It put a huge lump in Catriona's throat when Tilly and Suzy said exactly the same.

They waited until his family had given them one last wave before boarding the train; then Catriona realised with embarrassment that she was still holding Dominic's hand. Biting her lip, she gently released it.

'So that's the wedding done,' she said.

'And you can officially claim Lark Hill tomorrow,' he said.

'Thank you.' She took a deep breath. 'Your family are just so lovely. I can't believe your aunt made us that cake, and your uncle recorded a first dance for us.'

'I had no idea they were going to do that,' he said.

'We'll send flowers to your aunt,' she said, 'and a bottle of whatever your uncle's favourite is to him.'

'Bourbon,' he said, and grinned. 'Though I'd love to see you give him a lecture about how proper Scots single malt is better.'

'I'll remember to do that some time,' she promised. She looked at him. 'So I guess this is where we each get a taxi back to our own respective flats.'

'For a little while,' he said. 'With us having such a short reception, I thought today might feel like a bit of an anti-climax, so I booked us something for this evening. But we need to change out of our wedding clothes, first, otherwise you'll freeze.'

Weirdly, that felt as if he was cherishing her, and the lump was back in her throat. 'OK. I'll be guided by you,' she said.

'Just wear something warm. Layers. I'll come

over to pick you up,' he said. Then, to her surprise, he leaned forward and kissed her lightly on the mouth. 'You look stunning,' he said.

'You scrub up pretty well, too,' she said. 'And I noticed how your bow tie matches your buttonhole.'

'Couldn't let the Empress of Details down,' he said, and his eyes crinkled at the corners.

How had she ever thought this man dislikeable?

'I'll call you a cab,' he said, and flicked into the app on his phone. 'OK. It's on its way. I'll wait with you, and then I'm getting the tube to my place. I'll text you when I leave for yours.'

It didn't take long for the cab to come.

If the cabbie thought it strange that a bride would be on her own in the cab in her wedding dress, he didn't say anything. Though his rueful, 'Good luck, love,' made her wonder.

But a kiss, a first dance and a bit of cake didn't make their wedding real, she reminded herself. This was all part of a business deal. Dominic had his partnership, and she had her castle. End of story.

She changed into jeans and a long-sleeved T-shirt with another sweater over the top, took off her make-up, and carefully removed the hair vine Lou had woven through her hair, putting it back in its box. But she kept the pendant on, because it made her feel special.

Her phone beeped, and she picked it up, expecting a message from Dominic; instead, it was Ginny, sending her the photos and videos from their wedding day.

She leafed through them. They'd definitely convince her, she thought. The two of them standing in front of the registrar, looking nervous. Dominic gazing into her eyes as he slid a wedding ring onto her finger. Dominic kissing her. The two of them laughing as confetti floated down over them. Cutting the cake. Dancing together.

The kissing and the closeness they'd practised had definitely done the trick. They looked comfortable with each other. Close. Like lovers…

Except they weren't really lovers. Luke had made it clear she wasn't good at relationships. It was his excuse for cheating on her, to find the warmth that she lacked.

Maybe she should text Dominic and tell him that she had a headache and she'd see him tomorrow.

On the other hand, he'd clearly gone to some trouble to arrange something for this evening, and it would be rude and churlish of her to turn it down. Not to mention the fact that she'd discovered she actually wanted to spend time with him.

She'd just finished a mug of camomile tea when Dominic texted her. 'Five minutes.'

She was ready outside to meet him. He wouldn't tell her where they were going, but eventually they ended up at Greenwich, on a shuttle minibus to the Observatory.

'The Planetarium at night?' she asked, surprised.

He nodded. 'It's something I've always wanted to do. See the stars properly, and this is the best place in London.'

She knew somewhere better. 'The stars look amazing at Lark Hill,' she said. 'Keep your fingers crossed for a clear night, this week.'

'Have you got a telescope?' he asked, looking intrigued.

'No. But we can get up on the roof,' she said. 'And we might see meteors. Or the Northern Lights, if we're really lucky.'

'That would be amazing.' He grinned. 'I'll hold you to that.'

He held her hand all the way through the lecture, and then they looked at the stars through the telescope together. Dominic's pleasure in the stars was infectious, and Catriona enjoyed every minute.

When the event was over, they ended up walking along the river at Greenwich, their arms wrapped round each other, enjoying the Christmas lights. Strictly speaking, they didn't need to practise being comfortable together anymore: they were married. But she was enjoying the closeness, so she didn't pull away.

Back at Primrose Hill, Dominic kissed her goodnight on the doorstep.

Catriona almost, *almost*, asked him to come in. To stay.

But what if he turned her down?

Not wanting to take the risk, she said, 'Thank you for this evening. I'll pick you up at ten tomorrow.'

Was that disappointment or relief she could see in his face? She was good at reading clients, but utterly hopeless when it came to Dominic.

'Goodnight, Catriona,' he said. 'See you tomorrow.'

She stared at herself in the mirror as she brushed her teeth. Married. She didn't look any different. Didn't *feel* any different.

Except.

She couldn't get over the way his family seemed to have taken her to their hearts.

'Be sensible,' she reminded her reflection out loud. 'You're going to have a week's honeymoon—which will be spent working—and then Dominic's going back to London. You'll apply for a quiet no-fault divorce next Christmas. And that's an end to it.'

She slept badly that night, but a cool shower and washing her hair made her feel better, and coffee had her back to normal. Almost.

She drove to Islington to pick Dominic up, and he put a small case into her car. Clearly he was the sort to travel light.

'So tell me more about the castle,' he said as they left London behind.

She gave him a quick potted version of the castle's four hundred years of history.

'And does it get its name from larks who nest there?' he asked.

'The hill itself is in the shape of a lark—though actually that's pareidolia,' she said.

'I'm going to have to look up that word,' he said. 'That's the thing about you, Catriona. You make me think.' He fiddled with his phone. 'You mean it's like the face on Mars that isn't really a face. Cydonia.'

'Something like that,' she said. 'The idea is that the slope of the hill is the back of the bird, and the castle's the head.'

'Pareidolia.' He savoured the word. 'I'm so getting that word into my next report.'

'Seriously? In a legal report?' She laughed. 'I'd like to see that.'

'Challenge accepted,' he said with a grin. 'You'd better think up a good reward.'

Oh, the pictures that put in her head. She was

glad to have the excuse of needing to concentrate on driving, because no way she was telling him what she was thinking.

They shared the driving, but outside of London it quickly grew foggy; the journey dragged on, making both of them tired.

Catriona glanced at the clock. 'I can't believe how long it's taken us to drive here. It's taken us more than twice the time it usually would.'

'How far have we got to go?' he asked.

'We've gone past Durham; that's two hours or so from Lark Hill in normal weather. Except obviously today's not normal.'

'And driving in fog is driving me insane. I vote we stop and stay somewhere overnight, get some rest and hope it's better weather tomorrow,' he said.

'There's a motorway service station coming up. We could stop there and see if there's a hotel and they have a couple of rooms?' she suggested.

But everyone else had obviously had the same idea, because of the weather. 'I'm sorry. I can only offer you one room,' the receptionist said. 'And it's a double, not a twin.'

'We'll take it,' Dominic said. 'Thank you.'

They took their cases to their room, and Catriona called Mrs MacFarlane to let her know the weather was bad so they were staying at a roadside motel and would be at Lark Hill late tomorrow morning. They ordered room service pizza on the grounds they were too tired to move.

'Do you want the first shower?' Catriona asked when they'd finished eating.

'I'll be a gentleman and let you go first,' he said.

She showered as quickly as she could, and changed into her favourite pyjamas: a navy vest top and long navy pyjama pants covered in tiny white daisies. She discovered that Dominic's preferred nightwear was a faded band T-shirt teamed with jersey shorts.

'You look all in,' he said. 'Early night?'

'Early night,' she agreed.

He switched his phone to a playlist of soothing classical music; they climbed into bed, made sure there was the biggest possible gap between them, and Catriona closed her eyes in the hope that he'd think she'd fallen asleep almost immediately.

She woke a couple of hours later to discover that she was wrapped in Dominic's arms, and her hands were under the T-shirt he wore as a pyjama top, her palms flat against his back.

If she had any common sense, she'd untangle herself and move to the edge of the bed again; but instead she found herself snuggling closer.

He shifted and moved closer so his cheek was

against hers, then dropped a sleepy kiss on the corner of her mouth.

The next thing she knew, they were kissing—really kissing.

Then he stopped. 'I know we're married, but this wasn't the deal.'

Of course he didn't want to get closer to her. Hadn't she learned from Luke how bad she was at relationships? She shrank inwardly, feeling gauche and stupid and hideously embarrassed.

Her misery must've communicated itself to him in the way she held herself, because he kissed the corner of her mouth again. 'By that I mean, I don't want to take advantage of you—and I also don't have any condoms.'

'I'm on the pill,' she blurted out. 'Not because I sleep around, but because my periods are horrible.'

'I definitely don't think you sleep around,' he said, 'and, just so you know, I don't, either.'

It must've been a combination of strain and lack of sleep affecting her brain, because she said, 'So there's no reason why we couldn't…'

He went very still. 'Are you saying…?'

In answer, she lifted her hand and stroked his face.

He twisted his head and pressed a kiss into her palm.

She kissed his mouth.

He sighed her name and kissed her properly.

She couldn't remember the last time she'd been kissed like this, and white-heat desire shimmered through her. All she was aware of was Dominic: the warmth of his body, the way his hands felt against her skin, the thud of his heartbeat. She wasn't sure who removed whose clothes, or when, or how, but finally they were skin to skin—and it was oh, so good.

She gasped his name as he entered her. He went still for a moment, letting her adjust to the feel of him—and then he began to move, and every single thought went out of her head.

The next morning, when Catriona woke, she was still naked—as was Dominic. They were wrapped in each other's arms. And she didn't have a clue what to say.

'I didn't expect…' Her voice tailed off.

'I don't know how to behave with you this morning either,' he admitted. 'I think we were both tired last night—not thinking straight. We acted on…well.'

They'd acted on their instincts. On the attraction that had been growing between them ever since she'd first suggestion the marriage. Reacted with their bodies instead of their heads.

She took a deep breath. 'It's officially our honeymoon.' She paused. 'Maybe we could be honest about the fact that we…' She felt her face heat, but made herself continue through the ridiculous wave of shyness, 'That we're physically compatible. And we know this is a temporary thing. We could…enjoy each other's company.'

Echoing colour slashed across his cheeks. 'For a week.'

Was he going to turn her down? She couldn't quite meet his eyes. 'We could call it honeymoon privileges,' she mumbled.

'So I get to wake up with you in my arms for a week.'

Was that a hint of longing she could hear in his voice? So he wasn't pushing her away? Relief surged through her, followed by an urge to tease him. 'Unless I wake first.'

'Quibbled like a lawyer.'

She grinned. 'Well, Fergus. That's what we both are.'

'Honeymoon privileges. I like that idea.' He kissed her again. 'In fact, my dear Fifi, I like it a lot.'

Enough for them to be too late for breakfast, and they ended up having to get bacon rolls and coffee from the service station.

'This isn't quite the sort of breakfast I should be offering a viscountess,' he said.

'There's nothing wrong with a bacon roll,' she

said. 'Though I admit I usually have porridge for breakfast.'

'Even at Lark Hill? I expected you to have a breakfast room with a sideboard and silver salvers.'

'We do.' She might as well tell him the rest of it and get it over with. 'As well as a dining room, a drawing room, a morning room, a ballroom, the library and the study. But they don't all get used. It's too expensive to heat enormous rooms that aren't in use all the time,' she said. 'The kitchen, the morning room and Gramps's study are all we heat on the ground floor, and the bedrooms that are in use on the first floor.'

'How many bedrooms are there?'

'Six on the first floor.' Honesty compelled her to add, 'More on the second. A couple more reception rooms.'

He blinked. 'The castle has three storeys?'

She squirmed. 'Yes. It's a castle, Dominic. They tend to be a bit on the big side.'

'I can't imagine living in a place with that many rooms.'

'Look, it's not as if we have an acres-long dining table wend sit at opposite ends and shout to each other during meals,' she said crossly. 'Well, we do have a big dining table,' she amended, 'but we normally eat in the kitchen.'

'Right,' he said.

'A couple of centuries ago, you needed something that big because people came to stay for house parties and you needed the space to accommodate them all and their personal servants.' His raised eyebrows made her wince. 'Think about it. Back then, everything was done by hand. Imagine all the dust a coal fire produces—and how long it'd take to sweep a carpet or a floor instead of vacuuming. You'd need a lot of people to get everything done.'

'I guess,' he said. 'So Mrs MacFarlane lives in?'

'Yes. Though she's not a servant, and I don't expect her to wait on me. She's a very valued member of the household.' She narrowed her eyes at him.

'Got it,' he said. 'And she's the only one who works in the house?'

'She used to have help in the house when I was younger, because Lark Hill would be way too much for one person to manage, but the rooms we don't heat nowadays are dust-sheeted and only get a spring clean once a year. When, yes, we do hire in extra help.' She looked at him. 'Look, it's not a royal palace with sixty million rooms. It's the English equivalent of the Big House in the village.' She frowned. How had they managed to get from laughing about breakfast to arguing over her background?

'I'm sorry,' he said. 'I'm just trying to get my head round where you come from.'

'I'm just me,' she said.

'I don't mean to make you feel awkward. Actually, it's a bit daunting for me, going to your family's castle. My family live in ordinary houses. I'm the odd one out with the flashy flat in London.'

'You earn every penny of your salary,' she said. 'You've worked hard. You made partner on merit, not from social connections. That's something to be proud of.'

'Careful, Fifi. It sounds as if you're on Team Ferrars.'

'Maybe,' she said, 'I am. Just as you're on Team Findlay.'

He raised his mug in a toast. 'Team Us.'

'Team Us.' She took a sip of her coffee. 'Now the fog's cleared, it'll be a nice drive this morning, with the hills on one side and the sea on the other. You do the first half,' she said, 'because I know the road and it'll be a chance for you to enjoy the scenery of the second half.'

'Deal,' he said, and kissed her.

CHAPTER NINE

DOMINIC ENJOYED DRIVING along the coast. Catriona had been right about it being a pretty route; there was a touch of frost on the grass, and everywhere sparkled. They stopped halfway to grab a coffee, stretch their legs and for Catriona to text Mrs MacFarlane with their expected time of arrival, and then she took over the driving.

As she turned off the main road, he could see a hill and a castle in front of them. Clearly you could see for miles from the castle, too; back in the day, it would've been a good defensive position. 'I assume that's Lark Hill?' he asked.

'Yes.'

A short time later, she pulled into an entrance and stopped in front of a pair of ornate, heavy iron gates. He helped her open them, and then closed them behind the car after she'd driven through.

The driveway went up the hill, which wasn't quite as steep as it had seemed from the distance.

At the top was a green oval lawn, with deep shingle surrounding it and the castle.

'It was originally a carriage drive,' she said. 'It's easier to turn a horse and carriage round in a circle. We still have the old stable blocks, though they've been used as storage for years. Grannie rode when she was younger, but I don't ever remember horses being here.'

'That's a stunning building,' he said, staring at the castle. The three-storey square building was built of honey-coloured stone, with turrets at all four corners, the windows were tall sashes painted white, there was a porch jutting out with a large archway, and four stone steps that led to a wide, glossy black door.

She parked next to the house; they took their cases out of the car and walked up the steps. She opened the door to reveal a wide stone-flagged entrance hall; in front of them was a sweeping staircase up to the next floor.

Catriona called out, 'Mrs Mac?'

A woman he judged to be in her late fifties bustled into the hall and greeted her with a smile. 'Catriona, hen, I'm so glad you're home safely. I was worried about you yesterday in all that fog.'

'Thankfully it's a better day for driving today,' Catriona said, smiling back. 'Mrs Mac, I'd like to introduce you to my husband, Dominic Ferrars. Dominic, this is Mrs MacFarlane, our housekeeper. Or Mrs Mac to me, since I was very small.'

'Welcome to Lark Hill, Mr Ferrars.' Mrs MacFarlane greeted him with a warm handshake. 'Now, the kettle's on, I'll make coffee. Or tea, if you prefer.'

'Coffee would be lovely, thank you,' Dominic said, 'but please call me Dominic and I really don't expect you to wait on me.'

'Whisht, it's my job,' Mrs MacFarlane said, but she looked pleased.

'We'll take turns in cooking,' Catriona said, 'and the washing up is our job, not yours.'

'We'll discuss that later, hen,' Mrs MacFarlane said. 'I made soup and bread this morning for lunch. I thought I'd cook salmon for dinner tonight.'

'Thank you, that's perfect,' Catriona said.

'I assumed you'd want to be in your room rather than the master suite,' Mrs MacFarlane said, 'so I made up the bed there.'

'Thank you. That's perfect. Apart from the fact that it would feel odd to be in Gramps' and Grannie's room, my room has a better view,' she said. She looked at Dominic. 'Let's take our cases up, and then I'll give you the grand tour. Mrs Mac, did the valuers send the report through?'

'It's on your gra—*your* desk, in the study, hen,' the housekeeper corrected herself.

'Valuers?' Dominic asked.

'For the inheritance tax,' Catriona said, 'and I asked them to take note of the work that needs doing, so hopefully they've assessed the roof, the heating and the bit of damp I've been worrying about in the boot room.'

Boot room? It was the first he'd heard of it. How many more rooms were there she hadn't told him about?

She hefted her suitcase. 'Right—follow me.'

Her room was at the back of the castle, on the first floor. The first thing he saw was a king-sized four-poster bed in dark wood, with a solid headboard that stretched halfway up the walls, an ornately carved post at each corner and deep red velvet curtains.

'Do they go all the way round when they're closed?' he asked, indicating the curtains.

'They do indeed,' she said, 'which is very good in winter because it keeps the warmth in.'

There was a large wardrobe, a bookcase and a chest of drawers on one wall, a dressing table in front of the window, and a table with a lamp each side of the bed. In the middle of the dark oak floor was a thick pile rug, the sort that you weren't allowed to step on in a stately home and that he guessed was worth a great deal of money.

In the corner of the room was a turret, which held a comfortable-looking sofa and a desk. He went over and glanced out. 'You have a turret in your bedroom.'

She winced. 'It's not that fancy.'

'Yes, it is. But what a view of the gardens and the sea. It's stunning.'

'Which is why it's the best room in the house.' She joined him at the window. 'Sadly, the gardens aren't like they were when Grannie was alive. We still have a gardener who cuts the lawns and does the pruning and weeding, but nobody's added to her rose garden or developed anything else. I kind of feel guilty we've let her lovely flowers go to a low-maintenance thing, but something had to give and Gramps was never really bothered about plants. We have photos somewhere of how they used to look.'

'It might be worth restoring them,' he said, 'because people will pay to visit gardens. And that leads to scope for a tea shop, even if it's a pop-up thing.'

'Definitely one to add to the list of potentials,' she said, 'but first I need to look at the roof, the damp and the boiler, and work out the order in which they need to be tackled. I might end up having to extend my sabbatical.'

'I know you could do the project-managing in

your sleep,' he said, 'but that's an awful lot of worry on your shoulders.'

She shrugged. 'It comes as part of the responsibilities, I guess.'

'Do you resent it?' he asked. 'Giving up everything you worked for?'

'In a way, yes,' she said. 'I'm good at my job and I would've made a good partner. But I'll do a good job here, too.'

'Is there a way you can do both?' he asked. 'Get Lark Hill up and running the way you want it, hire someone to manage it, and come back to London?'

'Maybe. Or I could switch my career path and become a judge,' she said. 'Work part-time here and part-time in court. But I've got time to think about that.'

It sounded to him as if she'd already put some thought into it.

And if she didn't come back to London…what would that mean for them? She'd said this morning about honeymoon privileges. What about when the honeymoon was over? Did she expect them to lead separate lives, or would she consider any kind of compromise? He had no idea what she wanted. He wasn't sure what he wanted, either. The day before their wedding, he would've said that they were about to embark on a marriage of convenience, and they'd have a quiet amicable divorce in a year's time.

Last night had changed everything. He hadn't expected making love with Catriona to be so amazing.

Leaving that thought to work itself out in the back of his head, he asked, 'So what's the plan for today?'

'Lunch,' she said. 'Then I'll give you a proper tour of the castle. And, if you don't mind, I'll be taking the probate survey with me to check they've covered everything.'

'Anything I can do to help?' he asked.

'Maybe cast your eye over the report and check if I miss anything,' she said.

Catriona Findlay didn't miss details, Dominic thought, but he smiled. 'Sure.'

After a lunch of excellent Scotch broth and home-made bread, Dominic went room by room with her through the house. As she'd said, most of the rooms were dust-sheeted. There were several windows that needed mending because the sashes had decayed, damp patches in some of the top rooms where guttering had broken so water dripped through the mortar and through the walls and a very suspiciously damp corner in the boot room, as well as the work on the roof that she'd mentioned.

'And this is where you come out to watch the stars?' he asked.

'When I was small, yes. Grannie would give me an oilcloth to sit on and a blanket to wrap up in,' she said. 'She taught me the constellations. But I haven't sat up here for years. I guess, now I'm older, I'm more aware of the risks. Actually, I think we'd get just as good a view from the turret, and it'd be safer.'

'Do you know a good tradesman who works with listed buildings?' he asked.

'Gramps has a list, I think,' she said. 'If they don't have all the specialties covered between them, I'm pretty sure one of them will be able to recommend someone.' She grimaced. 'The sooner I put this into in a list, the less daunting it's going to feel. And, talking of daunting, I'd better face the music and let my mother and the boys know that we got married yesterday.' She took her phone from her pocket, typed out a brief message, added some of the pictures Ginny had sent her of the wedding, and pressed 'send'.

That evening, he and Catriona were sitting in the morning room, going through the paperwork, when her phone shrilled.

'It looks as if the boys have all read their messages,' she said. 'They're video-calling me. A joint thing.'

'Do you want me to give you some privacy?' he asked.

'No. It's fine,' she said. 'I probably ought to introduce you to them.' She took a deep breath and answered the call. 'Good evening, Tom, Lachy and Finn.'

She sounded cool, calm and collected—but Dominic noticed that her free hand was clenched, betraying her tension.

'What the hell do you mean, you got married yesterday?' one of them asked, sounding aggrieved. 'Is this to do with the will?'

'Because it's the first we've heard of you even *dating*,' another said.

'Yeah. My mum said you'd do something like this, to cut us out of our rightful inheritance,' the third said.

Dominic was shocked by the aggression in their tone. Catriona was their older sister. His own family would never dream of talking to him like that. Part of him wanted to grab the phone and ask who the hell they thought they were; but Catriona needed support, not someone taking over and interfering. He moved closer to her, making sure he wasn't visible on screen, and laid his hand over her clenched fist briefly to let her know he was there and on her side.

'The timing of the marriage is to do with the will,' Catriona said. 'But my husband isn't.'

That was a bit of a grey area, Dominic thought. Because their marriage *had* all been to do with the will…until last night.

Was she saying that she could see this being a real marriage? His heart beat a little bit faster at the idea.

Though right now wasn't the time to ask her about it.

'You sent pictures of you in a wedding dress,' the youngest said, 'but how do we know you didn't just dress up for it?'

'Yes. Where's the marriage certificate?' the oldest-looking brother asked.

'They're mailing it to me in the next ten working days,' she said. 'Which is standard procedure, so don't start thinking there's any conspiracy. And I wasn't dressing up, Finn. It was a real cake, a real first dance, and real signatures on the register in Camden. You're all perfectly welcome to check.'

There was general muttering from the three of them.

'In answer to your mother, Finn, I'm not cutting any of you out. My plan is to make sure you all get something. Before I can do that, I need to get the estate in a position where it's supporting itself and making money that I can split with you. I've spent this afternoon going over the probate inventory and checking what remedial work the castle needs, and tomorrow I'm seeing the tenants. And then I have the fun of going through the accounts. Unless any of you would like to offer help?'

The three of them were silent.

'I thought not,' she said. 'I'll send you the photographs I took this morning, and a copy of the probate inventory, so you can see it all for yourself how much work needs doing. But at least Gramps, unlike our father, left a will, which makes sorting everything out a lot easier.'

Between them, the brothers scoffed, rolled their eyes and muttered something Dominic couldn't quite catch.

'You're welcome to come and help with executor duties,' she said. 'Just let me know when you plan to arrive, and I'll get a room un-dust-sheeted for you.'

There was silence.

'In the meantime,' she said, 'let me remind you of our father. He died when you were fifteen, Tom; Lachy, you were ten; Finn, you were five. What do you remember of him?'

'The car he said I could have when I was grown up,' Lachy said. 'It was like James Bond's.'

'Hang on—he told me *I* could have the car,' Tom said.

'I don't remember the car. I don't really remember him very well, either,' Finn admitted.

'Because you were very young when he died, Finn,' Catriona said. 'I barely saw him after he left my mother for yours, Tom—which isn't a pop at you, by the way, it's just telling you how he was with me. Even before that, he and my mother used to drop me here at the castle so Gramps and Grannie could look after me while they jetted off to some Caribbean island for a party. Except the party would turn into quite a bit longer than a weekend.'

Dominic could see from their expressions that this was a revelation to them—and not a pleasant one.

'Dad used to turn up in that car,' Lachy said, 'and he'd take me out somewhere. He'd drive too fast, and we'd do all the things my mum wouldn't have approved of.' He frowned. 'And then I wouldn't see him for months.'

'Same here,' Tom said. 'Except he'd stay on the beach, drinking brandy and flirting with whoever was sitting near him, while I was surfing. He'd never come in the water with me.'

'I remember a trip to the zoo, and he bought me a stuffed tiger that was bigger than me,' Finn said.

'So what you're all saying is he didn't show his face often, and when he did he was larger than life?' Catriona asked.

Her half-brothers agreed.

'Our father,' she said, 'lived fast and died at the age of forty-nine, with four divorces behind him and no will. Sorting out his estate took me quite a lot of time.'

'I don't remember getting any money when he died,' Tom said. 'Unless you made sure any inheritance was tied up until my thirtieth birthday or something like that.'

'I couldn't have done that,' she said, 'and, besides, there wasn't any money. Because he was divorced and died intestate, we would've inherited everything equally between the four of us, but I'm afraid our father did everything on credit. A life of partying isn't cheap. Yacht hire, hotel bills—for a gaggle of hangers-on as well as himself—and the very best champagne,' she said. 'And I wouldn't be surprised if he'd been doing drugs as well. If I'd been Gramps, I would've cut off the funds and made him work. Given him a purpose in life, something to strive for.'

'And that's what you're going to do to us?' Tom asked.

'There *are* no funds for me to cut off, right now,' she said. 'And I'm afraid your mothers calling me a ball-breaker isn't going to conjure up a magic money tree.'

There were collective winces on the screen. 'You know about that?' Finn asked.

'I know everything,' she said tiredly. 'When

you're twenty-five years old and four women think you're holding out on them, they don't tend to mince their words.'

'Hang on. There are three of us. Or was your mum one of the four?' Tom asked.

'No,' she said dryly. 'My mother's independently wealthy. Or she was, until she developed a taste for expensive weddings and trading in the current spouse for a new model. Much like Dad.'

'So who was the fourth woman who had a go at you?' Finn asked.

'The woman he divorced your mum for, Finn. Except she had a miscarriage, or my guess is we would've had another baby brother.' She spread her hands. 'And he died before he could marry her, so she wasn't entitled to anything, even if there had been any money. She wasn't very happy about that.'

'Gramps left you everything,' Tom said. 'Is that because you're the oldest?'

'Without looking it up,' she asked, 'when was Gramps's birthday?'

The silence told Dominic that none of them had a clue. Which shocked him: he knew all the birthdays in his own family.

'Right,' she said dryly. 'Do you know mine? And don't start whining that women are the ones who sort that sort of thing out, and you're not girls.'

'No,' Tom admitted. 'But you always remember my birthday.'

'And mine,' Lachy agreed.

'And mine,' Finn said.

'So do you still all think I'm going to cut you off with nothing?'

There was another silence.

'Well, I'm glad I've embarrassed you into seeing the truth,' she said.

'The castle's going to be a money-pit,' Tom said. 'My best mate's parents live in a listed building that needed a new roof. It cost a fortune. And it took for ever to sort out.'

'Which is what I'm expecting to be the case here,' she said. 'But it needs doing. I think Gramps thought the three of you would sell up if he left it to you.'

'Of course we would,' Lachy said. 'You said there's damp, the roof needs fixing, and it needs a new heating system. It makes sense to let someone who actually likes doing that kind of stuff do it. Save yourself the hassle.'

'Lark Hill isn't being sold on my watch. Nor's any of the land,' she said. 'I'm selling some of the art to cover the inheritance tax, and I'll send you all a full record of what I do.'

'What about the tenants? Can't they pay more rent?' Tom asked.

'I'm not increasing the rents.' She blew out a

breath. 'Gramps taught me that with rights come responsibilities. We have a duty to our tenants to look after them, not fleece them.'

They said nothing for a while, as if digesting what she'd said.

'What about the new husband?' Tom asked. 'If he's real.'

'Ask him yourself.' She glanced at Dominic, who moved closer.

'Good evening. I'm Dominic Ferrars,' he said.

'And you married Catriona yesterday. How come none of us have heard of you before?' Tom asked.

'If you don't even know your sister's birthday,' Dominic said dryly, 'you're hardly going to know if she's dating someone.'

'How do we know you're not a gold-digger?' Lachy asked.

'You might want to check out how much a qualified senior solicitor earns in London,' Dominic said. 'And, if you all think that life's all about how much money you have, then I think you've got a fair bit of growing up to do.'

'Can we lower the testosterone level a bit, please?' Catriona asked, nudging him.

He smiled at her. 'Sure.'

'So how long have you been dating my sister?' Finn asked.

'I've known her for about seven years,' Dominic said.

'How do we know she didn't just marry you to get the castle?' Tom asked.

Dominic smiled, turned Catriona to face him and kissed her very thoroughly. 'That answer your question, boys?' he asked.

Finn pulled a face. 'That's so gross. Old people kissing.'

Dominic grinned. 'I'm twenty years older than you, yes, but that isn't *old*. And kissing isn't just for teenagers.'

'It's the first time I've seen Catriona blush,' Tom said.

'If you have anything constructive to say,' Catriona said, sounding cross, 'then I'll listen. Otherwise, I think we're done with this conversation.'

Tom shrugged. 'Whatever. Bye.' His part of the screen went blank.

'Yeah,' Lachy said. 'Bye.'

Which left Finn. Catriona was expecting him to flounce off, too, but instead he asked, 'Were you serious?'

'What? About being married to Dominic?' She rolled her eyes. 'I'll send you a copy of my wedding certificate, when it gets here.'

'No. I mean about helping. There are formal gardens at Lark Hill, right?'

'Which are not top of my priority list,' she said.

'You said you want to make the castle pay for itself,' Finn reminded her. 'People pay to visit gardens.'

'And you need public liability insurance for paying visitors. I need to cost it.'

'If the figures work,' Finn said, 'then I could come and look after the gardens.'

'Is that what you want to do with your career? Horticulture?' Dominic asked.

'Maybe,' Finn said.

'You're sixteen in April. You've got two more years at school,' Catriona reminded him.

'Two more years in *education*. It doesn't have to be at school,' Finn corrected. 'I could do an apprenticeship.'

'I'd need to discuss that with your mother,' Catriona said.

He sighed. 'So that's a no.'

'Your mother has parental responsibility for you until you're sixteen, Finn,' Dominic said, 'so we have to abide by her decisions. But if you want some help in finding information about a career in horticulture, we can do that.'

'Thank you,' Finn said. 'Lachy and Tom don't know I have a greenhouse. I don't want them taking the piss out of me.'

'Ignore them if they do,' Catriona said. She'd had no idea he was into gardening—and this was the first time he'd confided anything to her. She wanted to encourage him. 'What do you grow?'

'Chilis,' Finn said. 'If there's a decent-sized greenhouse at Lark Hill, I could probably grow enough to go into production. I was thinking Lark Hill chili sauce, made from Scotch Bonnets grown in Scotland. If you open the gardens to the public, that means you can have a tea shop and a plant shop—and you can sell home-made goods in the tea shop. Like my chili sauce.'

'That,' Catriona said, 'is going on my list of possible businesses. If you're serious about this, Finn, then I want you to write me a business plan.'

'I've never written a business plan,' he said. 'How do I do that?'

'Find a template on the internet,' she said. 'But make sure the source is sound.'

'Something from the government or a charity aimed at supporting businesses for under-twenty-fives would be a good start,' Dominic added.

'What if it's not good enough?' Finn asked.

'Then you'll learn where the gaps are and what you need to know to fix them,' she said. 'Rinse and repeat, until you get it right. Just like when you revise a subject for exams and work out where your gaps are. Just so we're clear, this isn't me being mean and refusing to help you; I want you to think for yourself and work out where you need to ask for help, because you'll learn a lot more that way than if I sit down and do it for you.'

'Got it,' Finn said, and gave her a genuine smile that took her breath away. 'If school was like you, I wouldn't hate it as much as I do.'

'I'll take that as a win,' Catriona said. 'Write me a draft plan. I'll see what we have here by way of greenhouses. And we'll look at your career options together.'

'Thank you,' Finn said. 'And…um…congratulations to you both on the wedding. And I'm sorry I wasn't very nice to you. I'll send you that plan tomorrow, Catriona.' Awkwardly, he ended the call.

'I didn't expect that,' she said, looking thoughtful. 'It sounds as if the baby of the family might be growing up.'

Dominic rubbed a hand over his face. 'Even though he thinks I'm a potential gold-digger, and we're both ancient.'

'He was very grossed-out by you kissing me,' she said. 'But, actually, that was genius. I think that convinced them more than anything I said.'

'I see what you mean now about your family not being like mine,' he said. 'I assume your grandparents were a little less…' he paused as if searching for the right word '…combative?'

'They were. But they were quite reserved and formal,' she added, wanting to be truthful.

'I think Finn might come good.'

She shrugged. 'We'll see.'

'By the way, I didn't step in when they were giving you a hard time because I'm not going to insult you by playing the knight on the white charger,' he said. 'You don't need one. Half the barristers in London are terrified of you.'

She remembered what her sort-of stepmothers thought of her. 'Do you think I'm a ball-breaker?' she asked.

'You can be,' he said. 'But only when it's necessary, and I think it's because nobody's really been on your side before.'

'Uh-huh.'

'You're not a stereotype, Catriona. You're like Cleopatra with her infinite variety,' he said.

'That's how you see me?' She stared at him. '*Antony and Cleopatra* was my A level set text.'

'Mine, too,' he said. 'And, yeah, that's how I see you. Enobarbus the low-born soldier, seeing Antony's "enchanting queen". Because you are. Enchanting.'

She blinked away the tears that welled up from absolutely nowhere. 'I think that's the nicest thing anyone's ever said to me.'

'It's true,' he said.

'And you're not low-born.'

He stroked her cheek. 'Compared to you, I am. But I don't care about class, and I don't think you do, either.'

'It's who you are that matters, not where you come from,' she said.

'Agreed. Anyway, your team's growing. Me, Mrs Mac, and maybe Finn. We're going to fix Lark Hill. Together.'

The idea made her heart skip a beat. *Together.* She'd expected to have to struggle with Lark Hill on her own. And this definitely hadn't been in her bargain with Dominic.

Just for a moment, the strain across her shoulders eased and it felt less as if she was trying to climb out of a deep well.

'Now, do you need a glass of wine after that, or shall I make you some camomile tea?' he asked.

'Tea would be really lovely,' she said gratefully. 'Thank you.' Before he stood up, she took his hand and pressed a kiss into his palm before folding his fingers over the kiss. 'Dommy. Thank you for having my back.'

He brushed his mouth against hers. 'You're very, very welcome, Trina.'

CHAPTER TEN

'I LIKE HIM, HEN,' Mrs MacFarlane said the next morning, when Catriona came down to the kitchen. 'I suspected you might have married him just to meet that ridiculous clause your grandfather put in his will—but it's the real thing, isn't it?'

Catriona hated lying to someone she'd known for so long, but she didn't exactly have a choice. 'Mmm…' she said.

'You know, I've been thinking about it and I'm sure that's why your grandfather made that clause,' Mrs MacFarlane said. 'Because he was worried about you being on your own. He didn't have a love match with your grandmother, but things changed over the years. I think he wanted you to find someone who'd rub along with you, and then over time you'd learn to love each other.'

'Maybe,' Catriona said.

'He's a good man, your Dominic. He's grounded. And he notices the little things—like your chamomile tea, and the way you drink your coffee,' Mrs MacFarlane said.

'He's a lawyer. He's supposed to pay attention to detail,' Catriona said.

'But he sees *you*, hen,' the housekeeper said. 'Not professional you, not Viscountess you. The real you.'

And that was a seriously scary thought—because Catriona thought Mrs Mac might be right. Last night she'd gone to sleep in Dominic's arms; this morning, the first thing she'd seen when she'd opened her eyes was him. When they made love, she felt like a different person. Cherished, just the way he'd promised on their wedding day. Valued.

She pushed the thought away. That wasn't the deal she had with Dominic, and it wasn't fair to change the terms of their agreement now— no matter how much he tempted her. He had a life in London, with his dream job. She couldn't ask him to change the terms of their deal, give all that up for her and move even further away from the family he adored. She'd just have to be sensible and remember that this was for a week, not for ever.

Dominic charmed the tenants that morning and helped Catriona reassure them that there would be no immediate changes in the estate, and definitely no changes to the rent; though she was looking to make the estate pay for itself and she was interested in any ideas they had. At lunchtime, she showed him the path down the cliff to the beach belonging to the castle.

'Is this a private beach?' Dominic asked.

'Technically,' she said, 'but as far back as I can remember we haven't minded the locals walking here. All we ask is that people take their litter home with them.'

'So you could go swimming in the sea every day.'

'You *could*,' she said, smiling. 'But at this time of year the water's about eight degrees centigrade. I don't think I'd even paddle at the edges, let alone swim properly.' She gave him a sidelong look. 'Of course, should you wish to accept a challenge…'

He laughed and kissed her. 'No. My common sense just about outweighs my testosterone.'

Later that afternoon, they took pictures of the gardens and the greenhouses for Finn, and had a chat with the gardener about what kind of practical experience Finn could get at Lark Hill and how it would work with an apprenticeship. She sent the photographs to Finn, who emailed her a business plan in return.

She read through it swiftly. 'It's pretty good for a first attempt,' she said, passing it to Dominic.

'He's taken what you said on board.' He looked approving. 'We've got time to review it and give him feedback, but then you need to go and change.'

'Change? Why?'

'I'm taking you out,' he said.

'Where?'

'I know you hate surprises,' he said, 'and so do I, but I promise you'll like this one.'

Taking her out. And this felt like a real date, so her stomach was filled with butterflies. He made her feel like a nerdy teenager being asked out by the hottest boy in school. 'What's the dress code?' she asked.

'Smart casual. We're having dinner, afterwards. Oh, but I think layers might be a good idea.'

Once they'd come up with a joint critique for Finn, she changed into black trousers and a pretty, long-sleeved top, wearing the pendant Dominic had bought her. He drove them into Edinburgh, with a bit of help from her satnav; she still didn't have a clue what he'd planned until he walked with her to St Mary's Cathedral. There was a candlelit piano recital, covering everything from Beethoven's 'Moonlight Sonata', Chopin and Rachmaninov through to Einaudi.

She held his hand throughout the performance, and this time it had nothing to do with looking comfortable with him and everything to do with the fact she wanted to do it.

Dinner afterwards was fabulous, too, in a

Georgian townhouse restaurant that specialised in seasonal Scottish food, and she enjoyed teasing him into trying haggis. They walked back through the streets to the Christmas markets; there were twinkling Christmas lights everywhere, the scents of orange and cinnamon and whisky floated in the air, and the street entertainers were singing Christmas pop songs—in some cases, accompanied by bagpipes.

Dominic nudged her. 'Hey. I knew I'd get my bagpipes fix.'

She laughed, and they paused to watch people at the ice rink.

'Do you want to have a go?' he asked, gesturing to the rink.

She shook her head ruefully. 'I'm afraid skating's not in my skillset. Don't tell me, you can do all the flashy jumps and spins?'

He laughed and kissed her. 'Skating's not in my skill-set, either. It's probably not going to be helpful if one of us ends up in plaster, is it?'

'Let's just explore the Christmas market,' she said.

'Sounds good to me,' he said. 'And I could do with getting some stocking-fillers for my family.'

It was perfect, wandering through the market with their arms round each other. Catriona was surprised and thrilled to discover that she actually felt like a newlywed—as if their honeymoon was real, particularly when Dominic stopped to kiss her under some mistletoe.

With some helpful suggestions from Catriona, Dominic bought some Scots cream liqueur for his mum and aunts and single malt for his uncles, wrist-warmers for his sisters, and he couldn't resist a soft toy shaped like a highland cow for his nephew Aiden.

He wanted to buy something for Catriona, but what did you buy a viscountess—let alone one who was trying to balance the family estate's books and whose home and office were so clutter-free that it was obvious she didn't like knick-knacks? He gleefully bought tartan wrapping paper. 'See. Told you, tartan's what the tourists look for up here,' he said.

She rolled her eyes. 'Next thing, you'll be wanting bagpipes lessons.'

'So I can serenade my sweetheart? Actually, hold that thought. And my shopping.' He left her with a bag for a second while he had a quiet word with one of the street bands to explain he wanted something special for his new wife, and gave a decent cash donation to their charity box. A few moments later, he returned. 'Right, wifey. Come with me.'

'Wifey?' she asked in mock outrage.

'That's my ring on your finger,' he said. 'Which makes you *ma noo wee wifey*.'

He deliberately hammed up the Scottish accent, and was rewarded with her laughing. 'That's terrible,' she said.

'You need some proper Gaelic lessons, laddie,' the piper of the band said, overhearing them. 'Is your lassie Scots?'

'She is,' Dominic confirmed.

'Right. Now, tell her *tha gaol agam ort*.'

'What does it mean?' Dominic asked. 'If I'm insulting her, I'm in trouble.'

'She'll know what it means, lad,' the piper said with a grin.

'*Ha geul ak-ham orsht*,' Dominic said, stumbling slightly over the pronunciation and needing a tiny bit of prompting from the piper.

Catriona went even pinker.

'And now you ask her,' the piper said, '*thoir pòg dhomh?*'

Dominic still wasn't sure if his leg was being pulled, but dutifully repeated, '*Hod pok goh?*'

'Go on, lassie,' the piper said. 'He asked you nicely.'

Catriona reached up on tiptoe and gave him a kiss.

Dominic grinned at the piper. 'Thank you. I'll remember that one.'

'You want to leave your shopping here?' the

piper asked. 'Because your new husband's asked for something special.' As soon as Catriona placed the bag by his feet, he winked at Dominic. 'Take it away, laddie.'

He began playing 'All I Want For Christmas Is You' on the bagpipes, and Dominic swept Catriona into his arms, dancing with her on the street and singing along to the song.

At first, she looked slightly panicky—and then, to his delight, she sang with him, relaxed into the dancing, and at the end of the song she kissed him.

'Merry Christmas,' the piper said when they collected their shopping.

'*Tapadh leat*,' Catriona replied with a smile.

'Thank you,' Dominic added.

The piper grinned. 'Your lassie's already said thanks. You have a nice night.'

'I had no idea you spoke Gaelic,' Dominic said to Catriona.

She shrugged. 'You never asked.'

'How many languages do you speak?'

'Including English and Gaelic?' She wrinkled her nose. 'Five. My German's a bit rusty, though.'

He should've guessed. Catriona was an overachiever all the way—though she didn't boast about it. 'My only other language is French,' he said, 'and that's seriously rusty. Still, I'll make a start on Gaelic. *"Hod pok goh"* is "kiss me", right? What was the rest?'

'Later,' she said, turning an even deeper shade of pink.

'I think,' he said, 'I'm going to enjoy Gaelic lessons. *Thoir pòg dhomh.*'

'You're getting very uppity, Mr Ferrars.' She grinned. 'Just wait until I make you spell it.'

'Then I'll need extra…' He paused. 'Which bit's "kiss"?'

'*Pòg,*' she said.

'Extra *pògs,*' he said, 'to encourage my diligence in studying and to reward my attempts at spelling a language that I'm guessing looks nothing like it sounds.'

She laughed, and kissed him.

And, as they walked through the streets of the city together, all felt very right in Dominic's world. He loved the vibrancy of the city; but, more than that, he loved the way the woman by his side continually managed to surprise him.

This wasn't meant to be a real honeymoon at the start of a real marriage; they'd agreed it was a temporary thing.

But what if it wasn't?

The closer Catriona allowed him to get to her, the more he found himself enjoying her company. A walk hand in hand by the sea, tasting the salt on her lips when he kissed her. A cosy dinner by the fire in the local pub. Sitting in her turret and watching the stars, seeing a meteor streaking past in the clear night sky.

'What did you wish for?' he asked.

'Can't tell you, or it won't come true,' she said with a smile. 'Which is why I'm not going to ask you, either.'

He was shocked to realise what he wished for: that their convenient marriage would become real. He'd never expected to do all the cosy couple stuff with her, and it was a revelation to him that not only did he enjoy it, he wanted to do a lot more of it.

But how did she feel about him? If he tried to woo her, particularly from a distance when he went back to London, would she push him away? Or would she try to find a compromise so they could be together?

He'd ask her…but he'd need to find the right moment.

Monday was dank and miserable, full of the kind of fine drizzle that had you soaked before you knew it. And it suited Catriona's mood. Today was the end of their honeymoon. Day seven of their marriage. She had to be honest with herself: it was also the end, because Dominic was flying back to London.

This near-week had been stolen out of their

lives, and it wasn't to be repeated—no matter how much she wished things could be different.

She'd booked a meeting with her grandfather's solicitor so she wouldn't have to stay and watch Dominic walk away from her. Though she was tempted to cancel it when he enveloped her in a bear hug. She didn't want to move out of his arms, ever again.

Though that wasn't the deal.

'I'll message you when I'm back in London,' he said.

'Safe journey,' she said, forcing herself to smile and hoping that she looked inscrutable rather than near to crying. 'I'm not very good at goodbyes. And I've got a meeting in the city centre.'

'OK. But before I go…' He leaned forward and kissed her. A kiss so sweet and yearning that it made tears glint in her eyes. But Dominic wasn't really hers. He was borrowed, and she had to let him go now.

'You'd better check in,' she said.

As soon as he'd taken his case out of her car and closed the boot, she raised a hand in acknowledgement and drove away.

Having to drive, even if it was only for half an hour or so, meant she couldn't indulge in tears; besides, she didn't want to turn up to a meeting with her eyes red and puffy. It would be unprofessional, and Catriona Findlay had the word *professional* practically stamped through her, like a stick of seaside rock.

She felt as brittle as a stick of seaside rock, too.

At least having all the paperwork to sort out meant that she could fill her time completely—and pretend she wasn't missing him.

She knew she'd been right not to give in to temptation when Dominic sent her an anodyne message to say that he'd arrived safely. Of course he wasn't going to tell her he loved her. He'd only said the words to her in Gaelic because the piper had coached him through it, and he hadn't known what he was saying. And of course he wouldn't miss her. He had a busy schedule and his promotion would be announced before Christmas.

Glad you had a good flight. CF, she replied.

She told herself she didn't miss him when she went to bed alone, that night.

She told herself she didn't miss him when she lay awake at three a.m., remembering how his touch had made her body feel as if it was singing.

She told herself she didn't miss him when she checked her phone for the umpteenth time to find no messages from him.

This was crazy, Dominic thought. Catriona had never spent the night in his flat. So why did his bed feel too wide?

A punishing workout in the gym at ridiculous

o'clock before work didn't help. The endorphins weren't enough to make up for her absence. And work felt as if he'd never been away: except he was keenly aware of the empty desk in the open-plan room.

How was he going to woo his wife from a distance?

Catriona wasn't like other women. A big, sweeping romantic gesture would be met with a raised eyebrow and a caustic remark. A small gesture, on the other hand—something with a bit of thought behind it—might produce a different result. He could still remember the delight on her face when he'd given her the pendant; she'd loved the fact that he'd had it made to match her grandmother's ring.

In his morning break, he went out for 'fresh air' and called an Edinburgh florist.

A little later on, Mrs MacFarlane came into the study with a mug of coffee and a beautifully gift-wrapped bouquet. 'Delivery from Edinburgh for you,' she said.

'Flowers?' Who would send her flowers? Nobody had ever sent her flowers, even Luke in the day when he'd tried to impress her.

The second she saw the flowers, she knew exactly who they were from. Gerbera—like the ones her wedding bouquet, except these were all bright, hot colours. Scarlet, in-your-face pink, yellow.

Only one person could've sent her these. The person who'd turned her world from monochrome to unexpected bright, hot colours.

'Thank you, Mrs Mac,' she said.

'From your young man, I'll guess,' Mrs Mac-Farlane said.

'Probably. They're lovely and bright.'

All part of the show, she told herself. He hadn't meant it.

Though the message took her breath away.

Fifi—hod pok goh—Fergus.

A tear spilled over her cheek, and she brushed it away. Ridiculous. She couldn't afford to be sentimental. Couldn't let herself hope that he meant any of it.

But she duly typed a message to him.

Thank you for flowers. A+ for colour and form. E- for spelling.

Unexpectedly, she had an immediate response.

Glad you liked them. How's it spelled, then?

No kisses. No sentimentality. Then again, she wasn't sentimental.

She messaged back.

Thoir pòg dhomh.

No WAY. How the hell was I supposed to get that? DH = G? Where does the M come in? And that D is in the wrong place. Huh. From Severely Sulking of London.

She typed back, grinning.

Attention to detail, my dear Fergus.

He was the only man she'd ever met who could make her laugh like this.

And you have no excuse for not checking the internet. You have good Wi-Fi in London.

He didn't reply, and it left her feeling flat.

Then again, she knew he was busy at work. Her own days in the office had been full. They were full here, too—but weirdly they felt empty without him.

The only other message she had that day was from her mother.

Congratulations on getting hitched. Will try to come over in summer to meet him.

Right, Catriona thought. It had taken Victoria nearly a week to reply to her message about the wedding, and they both knew that, even if her mother did make a firm arrangement to meet up, it would be cancelled at the last minute.

Catriona typed back That would be lovely, knowing perfectly well that it wouldn't happen. And she was so used to her mother that it didn't upset her any more.

On Wednesday morning, a package arrived with the label of a Borough Market stall. It was a piece of wrapped cheese, with a note in Dominic's distinctive handwriting.

Why is this package dangerous? Fergus

She thought about it for a good ten minutes before giving up.

All right. I'll bite. Why is the package dangerous?

He made her wait until lunchtime for the answer.

Because, my dear Fifi, it's a sharp cheddar.

She groaned, but the pun had amused her.

It's very delicious, actually. Eating it with some of Mrs Mac's chutney and good bread. PS Any pun you can do, I can do feta.

And she followed up with a little internet shopping, sending him a pair of socks decorated with bagpipes.

He didn't respond to her implied challenge, and she guessed he was in a meeting; she damped down the disappointment.

But she was surprised by emails later that afternoon from both Tom and Lachy. Lachy apologised for being snippy with her and offered to sort out a website if she was opening Lark Hill to the public or running events; and Tom suggested holding murder mystery weekends, adding that he'd be happy to act as a tour guide, because there was a good surfing beach just down the road and it might be fun to surf in Scotland instead of Cornwall.

Catriona thanked them both, and forwarded their messages, as well as her mother's, to Dominic.

He didn't reply until later that evening—which she guessed was after his usual family video call.

Glad Tom and Lachy are coming good. My mother and sisters send love. Saying nothing re your mother on grounds of least said, the better.

Just how she felt, too.

* * *

Dominic loved Catriona's cheesy puns.

Actually, if he was honest with himself, he loved her.

He wasn't quite sure when he'd fallen for her—before the wedding when she was trying to be brave, on the day of the wedding when she'd danced with him and watched the stars, or the day after the wedding when they'd both been so tired that their barriers had fallen apart and they'd taken comfort in each other.

He couldn't woo her with emails and texts. It wasn't enough. He wanted to be with her. Properly. As her legally wedded husband.

But.

He raked a hand through his hair. He'd always put his family first. Falling for Catriona meant there was someone else he'd have to consider. Someone else he'd need to put first.

Or maybe not. Because they'd all taken to her, and considered her to be part of them. He'd had messages from every single one of them telling him so—including from the ones who knew the truth about the wedding deal he'd made with his rival.

The only barrier to him telling her how he felt was Catriona herself. Because, if he'd got this wrong, she'd back away. She'd put an extra layer of metaphorical barbed wire under those painted hoardings to make him back off.

It was a risk.

A huge, huge risk.

Then again, not telling her would be worse. If he kept silent and simply gave her the divorce they'd agreed to in a year's time, he'd always wonder: what if he'd been brave enough to tell her how he felt and ask her to make their marriage a real one?

Not being with her because she didn't love him back would be hard. But it wouldn't be as hard as not being with her because he hadn't had the courage to challenge her.

This wasn't something he was going to do by text. He needed to see her eyes when he told her. There was nothing in his diary that couldn't be moved, and he had annual leave that needed taking. He'd sort it out in the morning—and then he'd book a flight to Edinburgh.

It was late the following evening when Catriona had a response to the socks.

Wonderful socks. Thx. I was thinking of having a tattoo, but worried you might complain about all the bagpipers.

She got the pun immediately.

Very good, Fergus.

Worth a pòg?

Definitely. And if only it could be in person. But that wasn't their deal.

A+ for spelling this time.

Trying to keep standards up. Cough. Where is my pòg?

X

Hmm. B- for effort.

<3 X <3

Improving. Still only B+. Try harder.

She could just see the teasing expression on his face as he typed, and longing flooded through her. But how could she tell him how she felt, when she knew they didn't have a future?

He didn't contact her on Friday or Saturday. But on Sunday afternoon, there was a knock on her study door, and a deep voice announced, *'Ma-tin va.'*

'Good morning', in Gaelic. In an utterly terrible accent, but he was clearly trying.

'Dominic?' Oh, and her voice *would* have to squeak. 'What are you doing here?'

'Come to claim my *pòg* in person.' He smiled. 'It seems I have a bit of time in lieu, so I thought I'd come and save you from drowning in paperwork.'

He'd taken some of his annual leave to help her? She'd never seen this kind of support in any of her parents' marriages, and she was at a bit of a loss how to react. She wanted to run to him, to throw her arms round him and kiss him until he was stupid; but another part of her remembered all the misery she'd seen in relationships. Her parents' constant divorces and remarriages, her own failed engagement. What was to say she'd manage to get this to work? The only marriage she'd seen working in her family was that of her grandparents—and they'd always felt emotionally reserved. So maybe that was just how things were for her family: the only way it could work was if you kept yourself aloof.

He coughed. 'Um… I even learned how to say "good morning" in Gaelic, just for you. *And* I can spell it.'

'I'll be the judge of that,' she said primly.

He came over to her and spun her round on her office chair. 'Oh, will you, Your Ladyship?'

And then *he* kissed *her* stupid.

'I missed you,' he whispered.

She'd missed him, too. Seeing him here again showed her just how much having him here with her made it feel as if the sun had pushed its way through the rain clouds and was making everything sparkle. She wanted to tell him that, but fear held her back. How could she trust him with her heart govern her feelings, when she knew love didn't last? Keeping him at arm's length was the only way to protect herself from the misery of it all going wrong.

He scooped her off her chair, took her place and settled her on his lap. 'So how's the paperwork?'

'Under control. How's the office?'

'Pretty much how you left it. Apparently your temporary replacement is joining us after Christmas.'

'And your promotion?'

'Announced,' he said. 'Last week.'

And he hadn't told her.

As if he'd guessed her feelings, he said, 'I didn't tell you because it still feels like rubbing your nose in it.'

'We had a deal,' she said. 'I have the castle. It would have been nice to know I held up my end of the bargain.'

He stroked her face. 'I apologise. I should've told you. And said thank you.'

'No need. It's what we agreed. Anyway, I had no

idea you were going to come here today,' she said. 'I would've met you at the airport, if I'd known.'

'I got a cab,' he said. 'I wanted to surprise you.'

'You certainly did that,' she said, smiling because, for the first time all week, she was genuinely happy.

The world felt back in kilter for Catriona, with Dominic back in the castle. Having someone to bounce ideas off, someone to encourage her in the good ideas and suggest alternatives for the ideas that didn't work. But, most of all, just him being there. Waking up with him in the morning, falling asleep in his arms at night, and even one evening spent on the roof, watching the stars and being thrilled to spot a meteorite.

'Wish on a falling star,' he said, 'but don't tell me or it won't come true.'

Even though she knew it was just a superstition and it wouldn't come true, she wished he could be hers for real. Except then she'd need a second wish to make sure it all worked out, rather than ending in disappointment.

But a couple of days before Christmas, he asked, 'What are your plans for Christmas?'

She shrugged. 'I always used to come here for a couple of days, so Gramps wouldn't be on his own. But he's not here, now. Mrs Mac went to her sister's yesterday. I guess I'd planned to treat Christmas like any other day and work through it.'

'What about Finn, Lachy, Tom and your mum? Aren't you planning to see them?'

'They're all doing their own things. I've sent cards and presents.'

'You could come and spend Christmas with my family,' he suggested.

A real family Christmas.

Dominic had already described it to her: how everyone got together in one place, bringing a dish to share. Crackers and paper hats, Uncle Bill leading the singalongs, games of charades, everyone noisy and laughing and together.

The sort of Christmas she'd never had.

The sort of Christmas that could capture her heart completely—then it would really hurt when she and Dominic divorced in a year's time, as planned. She realised then that if she let herself fall for him and his family, the divorce would leave her shattered. She needed to keep them all at arm's length, to protect herself.

'No, I couldn't,' she said.

'Why not?' he asked.

'I have things to do here.' She tried for a lightness she didn't really feel.

'On your own?' He raised an eyebrow. 'You're not going to be able to hold meetings on a bank holiday.'

'I can do other things. Prep work.'

'Is my family the problem?'

Yes, but not in the way he meant. 'No, of course not.'

'I don't get it. Talk to me, Catriona.'

That was just the thing. She couldn't. How could she even begin to explain all the mixed-up stuff in her head?

He blew out a breath. 'OK. I know you're twitchy about marriage and I know our deal's for a year. But I think things have changed between us over the last few weeks. So I'm going to take a risk and tell you how I feel. I've fallen in love with you, Catriona. I want this to be a real marriage. Obviously we've got things to sort out, with me being in London and you being here, but I think we can find some sort of compromise and make it work.'

He loved her.

He wanted a real marriage.

He was prepared to compromise.

But.

She'd tried before, with Luke, and it hadn't worked out. Her parents had never managed to make a marriage work. What was to say that she could make it work with Dominic? If she let him in and it all went wrong, she knew that this time she'd never recover.

'No,' she said lying through her teeth. 'That

isn't what I want.' It was everything she wanted—but she was too scared to take that risk.

'Are you telling me you don't feel the same?' he asked.

She dug her fingernails into her palm and lied again. 'Yes.'

'OK,' he said. 'No problem. I'll catch a flight and get out of your hair.'

She said nothing—and he left the room, closing the door very quietly behind him.

She knew he was going to pack. And then he'd be gone. Leaving her on her own, the way she'd always been.

It was her own fault. She'd pushed him away. He'd offered her his heart, and she'd been too scared to accept it for the precious gift it was.

She ought to go after him. Explain. Tell him she wanted him all the way back, but she was scared. And, every time she tried to find the right words to tell him, her mind froze.

And then it was too late.

He'd gone.

CHAPTER ELEVEN

How HAD HE got this so wrong? Dominic wondered. They'd got closer since their honeymoon. He'd missed her horribly in London—and he'd thought from her messaged that she'd missed him, too.

What an idiot he'd been. The one woman he'd actually discovered he wanted to be with…and it turned out that she didn't feel the same about him. He'd made a deal with her, and she wanted to stick with it. No changes and no compromises—because she didn't love him. Didn't want him.

Her silence when he'd offered to get out of her hair had made him feel as if he'd just dropped down to the bottom of a deep well. The sunlight he'd felt around her had been sucked into a black hole.

It was the first time he'd ever offered his heart to someone—and, instead of accepting it or behaving as if it was something special—she'd thrown it back at him. Smashing it into tiny pieces; every shard had lodged in his skin, stinging and burning.

The cab driver gave up trying to make conversation with him, and Dominic remained sunk in misery all the way to the airport. He didn't want to go back to London, either. He wanted to be with people who loved him. The place he knew he'd be accepted, and where they'd made him talk until all the hurt came out and he could heal.

Though he wasn't sure his heart would ever heal. It was in too many pieces.

Thankfully he managed to get a flight which meant he wouldn't have to hang around the airport for hours, seeing the kind of joyful reunions he'd hoped for and hadn't got. He used noise-cancelling headphones on the plane to make sure nobody talked to him, and again in the taxi once he'd given the address to the driver.

And then he rang his mother's doorbell.

'You look terrible, Dommy,' Ginny said. 'And why didn't you say you were coming? Where's your car?'

'I didn't drive,' Dominic said. 'I flew.'

'From London? Surely the train's easier?'

'From Edinburgh,' he admitted.

She frowned. 'Then where's Catriona?'

'I…' He blew out a breath. 'Mum, it's such a mess.' He filled her in on the honeymoon that had turned his convenient marriage into a real one. 'I fell in love with her, Mum. I thought we had a future. But she doesn't love me back.'

'Are you sure about that?' Ginny asked.

'Yes. I told her how I felt. She said she didn't feel the same.'

Ginny frowned. 'Maybe she wasn't telling you the truth. Take another look at your wedding photos. What I see is a bride in love with her new husband.'

He flicked through the pictures. His bride walking down the aisle to him. The shyness on her face. Confetti. The glint in her eye when she'd thrown the bouquet straight to Lou. Cutting the cake. Dancing with him.

'We were playing a part,' Dominic said. 'It was all part of our wedding deal. It wasn't real.' He shook his head. 'At least, it wasn't supposed to be. Maybe I ought to go back to London and work through Christmas rather than ruin it here for everyone.'

'We'll all be worrying about you even more if you do that,' Ginny said. 'Stay. We can't fix this for you, but we're your family and we love you.'

'Love you, too,' Dominic said. He just wished that Catriona had been able to love him as well.

Pride wasn't a good substitute for the man you'd fallen in love with and pushed away, Catriona thought, wide awake at ridiculous o'clock in the morning.

Maybe she'd been wrong.

Maybe this whole thing with Dominic could

have worked out. Hadn't she chosen him as her temporary groom in the first place because he had integrity? Her relationship with him wouldn't have ended up the same way as her parents, split after split after split, because he wasn't like them.

But she hadn't given them the chance. She'd pushed him away.

As she was the one who'd called a halt, it stood to reason that she was going to have to be the one to go after him. Be honest with him.

But first she had to find him.

Catriona threw the covers back and dashed round the room, getting dressed.

Had he gone back to London, or to Birmingham?

In the bathroom, she splashed her face with water. Now wasn't the time to give in to stupid emotions. She needed to think about this logically. It was Saturday. Christmas Eve was tomorrow. So the odds were that he'd chosen Birmingham—or, if he hadn't, he'd be there tomorrow.

She waited until it was a reasonable time of the morning, and texted Ginny.

Sorry to message you so early, but is Dominic with you?

To her relief, the reply came straight away.

Yes.

Please can you keep him there? I need to talk to him, but it has to be in person.

Of course.

And please don't tell him I'm coming.

She checked flights on her laptop. Thankfully there was still a seat on the plane. She booked it, and a cab to get her to the airport, then packed an overnight bag that wouldn't need to go in the hold. If she couldn't fix things with Dominic, she'd find a hotel for the night, or just hire a car and drive back to Lark Hill.

She couldn't settle to anything before the taxi arrived. Every time she glanced at her watch, convinced that minute must've passed, she was shocked to see it was a handful of seconds. But finally she was at the airport.

Her nerves felt as if they were screwing more and more tightly in her stomach, the nearer they got to Birmingham. She was nearly sick when the plane landed, and barely managed to mumble the right address to the cabbie.

And then she was there. Outside the front door.

This was it.

Make or break.

When Dominic would reject her—or maybe not.

Swallowing hard, she rang the doorbell.

And her knees went weak when he opened the door.

Dominic's breath caught. 'Catriona. What are…?' He stopped. She looked uncharacteristically nervous, and as if she wanted to run away. Asking questions might make her do just that, and he didn't want to take that risk. Not if there was a chance that they could have the conversation they should've had in Scotland. 'I didn't expect to see you,' he said instead. 'Would you like to come in?'

She looked as if the words had frozen in her head and she couldn't answer.

'On second thoughts, let me grab a coat and we'll go to the park, so we can have a private conversation,' he said. 'Leave your bag here.'

She nodded, still saying nothing, and he took her bag. He left it neatly in the hallway and grabbed his coat. 'Just going out for a bit, Mum,' he called, not waiting for the answer.

He led her over to the park; it was half an hour before sunset, so it was almost deserted and it was easy to find an empty bench.

'I'm sorry,' she said. 'I… I'm not good at this sort of thing. I messed up. Badly. And I'm sorry I hurt you.'

'Yes, you hurt me,' he said. 'I'm not in the habit of declaring myself.'

'The words got stuck,' she said. 'I wanted to say yes.' She took a deep breath. 'I want to spend Christmas with you, Dominic. I don't care whether it's here, or London, or Lark Hill—as long as I'm with you. Remember that night we saw the falling star?'

He nodded. Now she was talking, he didn't want to interrupt and give her the chance to clam up again.

'I wished our marriage was a real one. Not like my parents, getting bored and moving on all the time, but a real one—a forever marriage.'

'Me, too,' he said. 'I wished it was real.'

Her eyes were shining with a mixture of delight and disbelief.

'That night in Edinburgh, when the piper made you say things to me in Gaelic: I'm going to be brave and say it to you now. *Tha gaol agam ort.*'

'What does it mean?' he asked, even though he was pretty sure he'd worked it out for himself.

'I love you,' she said simply. 'I don't know how or when or where it happened, but I do. I love you. Dominic—and I really don't know what to do about it. I grew up not knowing what love looked like—I mean, I know my grandparents grew to love each other, but they were from a different generation. I don't know how to deal with this. What to do. What to say.'

The searing honesty made him want to weep for her.

'Just as well I know what to do about it,' he said. '*Tha gaol agam ort*, Catriona. If I'd known what I was saying that night, I would've told you again in English so you knew I meant it. Because I love you, too. I can't remember when I fell for you, either, but it feels like it's always been you. That you were the one I was waiting for.'

'That's how I feel about you,' she said. 'I want our marriage to be real. So much. But…' She shook her head. 'How are we possibly going to make it work? Lark Hill's hundreds of miles away from your job. As the newest partner, you'll hardly be able to do remote working.'

'About that,' he said.

Her eyes narrowed. 'What?'

'I told Lewis I think they have room for two new partners. One who's good at strategy, and one who's good at details. Dream team. You and me.'

Her eyes went wide. 'What did he say?'

'He agreed. When you're back from sabbatical, they'll ask you.'

'Oh, Dommy,' she said.

He grinned. 'I love it when you call me that. When you lose the starch. When your voice goes that little bit breathy.' At the thought of the last time she'd called him that, his pulse started racing. 'You make me hot all over.'

Her face went pink. 'You make *me* hot all over.'

'We fit,' he said softly. 'And, yes, we'll have to work at it, but we'll make everything work out because we're a team. We can do this: together.'

She lifted her chin. 'I can sell Lark Hill. Let someone else look after it.'

He shook his head, knowing that wasn't what she really wanted. She loved the place. 'It's your family heritage. I can't let you do that.'

'How else can we make it work?' she asked.

'We can spend half the time in London, half the time at Lark Hill.'

'Not half and half. We need time here, too,' she said. 'I want to be part of your family. Even though I'm not good at family stuff.'

'We'll teach you,' he said. 'And then you can teach your brothers how to be a family.'

'Ha——' She stopped herself mid-correction. 'My brothers,' she confirmed. 'I can get to know them and make a family with them. Trust them to help me make Lark Hill work.'

'We can have it all,' he said. 'And maybe, if we're lucky, we'll add to our family. I always thought I never wanted children, because I had responsibilities at a very early age—but being with you has changed my mind.'

'What if I'm a terrible mother?' she asked.

'You won't be,' he said. 'You'll be the kind of mother you wanted to have, not the one who let you down. Remember, your grannie loved you. I gather she was a bit reserved, but you knew deep down she loved you.'

She thought about it. 'You're right. And Mrs Mac thinks that's why Gramps put that clause in his will. Because he didn't marry Grannie for love, but they learned to love each other. So if he made me find someone I could work with as a team, over time we'd learn to love each other.'

'Over time,' he said.

She nodded. 'And I have. Just…quicker than I thought it would happen.'

He stroked her face. 'Me, too. You're my heart,' he said.

'*Mo cridhe*,' she said.

'*Mo credi-eh*,' he repeated. 'Which is?'

She smiled. 'What you said.'

He grinned. 'Well, now. My third Gaelic phrase, and I said it correctly.'

She grinned back. 'I have a feeling I know what my husband's going to say next.'

'Couldn't be anything else, could it?' he agreed, his smile broadening. '*Thoir pòg dhomh.*'

And she did.

EPILOGUE

Two years later

'IF YOU'D TOLD me two years ago that we'd be spending Christmas and New Year at Lark Hill with our entire families, I would've scoffed,' Catriona said. 'Yours, maybe—but not mine.'

The ballroom was decked out for Christmas and New Year, with a huge fir tree covered in pretty baubles. Lachie had set up a sound system playing music that would appeal to everyone from Finn to Mrs Mac, and everyone was dancing. Including the tenants and their families, her brothers' mothers and their new partners. Catriona's own mother wasn't there, but it didn't matter any more. There were more than enough people who wanted to be here with her. The family she'd always longed for—even her sort-of stepmothers.

'If you'd told me two years ago that Mum would finally marry Ray, I would've scoffed,'

Dominic said. 'But she said we inspired her to be brave.'

'They look so happy together,' Catriona said. 'And the boys have all come good.'

'Because you gave them the chance to run with their own ideas,' Dominic said. Finn was doing his apprenticeship as a gardener, and had got their grandmother's flower garden back to its original gorgeous design. Lachie was in charge of finance, and had set up the barns to start production of Lark Hill oat-based toiletries, as well as Finn's chili sauce, with the help of the tenants. The castle's tearoom showcased local artists, and everything in the gift shop was produced locally. Tom still surfed for fun—but he'd really come into his own, managing the staff and the visitors. The new biomass boiler had been installed and worked well, the leaky roof was fixed, and the whole summer was booked up with weddings.

'I'm just glad that they see Lark Hill for what it is,' she said. 'And I think Gramps and Grannie would've really approved.'

'Would they have approved of me?' Dominic asked.

'Oh, yes. And Grannie would've wanted you to do exactly what you're going to do in—' she glanced at her watch '—actually, right now. Go and walk round the gardens for five minutes.'

'It'd be nicer if my wife walked with me. So I could kiss her in the snow,' Dominic said.

'Not for first-footing,' she said. 'It's hugely unlucky for a woman to be the first-footer.'

He grinned. 'You could start a new tradition.'

'Nope. We need a tall, dark-haired man. That's you. *Go.*' When he made no move, she rolled her eyes. 'You can kiss me as much as you like in the snow afterwards.'

He drew her closer, and whispered in her ear, 'I'm so holding you to that. Lots and lots of *pògs*, Fifi.'

She grinned. 'Lots and lots. Now, off you go. You know the rules—you have to leave the house before the first strike of midnight. And everything's ready on the kitchen table.'

Of course it would be ready. Catriona would never leave a detail off her list.

When Dominic walked into the kitchen, on the table there was a coin, bread, a small jar of salt, a lump of coal, and a miniature bottle of whisky, to represent all the things they could wish for in the new year: prosperity, food, flavour, warmth and good cheer.

But the bit that Dominic was looking forward to most was claiming his kiss from the viscountess. No, not the viscountess—*his* viscountess.

He shrugged on a coat, gathered up the first-footer gifts, and strolled around the castle until the windows opened—another Scottish new year tradition—and he could hear the countdown to new year.

Once the chimes of midnight had finished, he knocked on the front door.

Catriona opened it, and he could hear everyone singing 'Auld Lang Syne' very loudly.

'Welcome,' she said.

'May this house always be warm,' he said, handing over the coal. 'May there always be food on the table.' He gave her the bread and the salt. 'May the family of this house and all visitors be blessed with good health and prosperity.' He handed over the coin and the whisky and smiled. 'And now I claim my kiss…'

* * * * *

*If you enjoyed this story,
check out these other great reads
from Kate Hardy*

**Tempted by Her Fake Fiancé
Crowning His Secret Princess
One Week in Venice with the CEO
Snowbound with the Brooding Billionaire**

All available now!